JOURNEY OF THIEVES

LEGENDS OF DIMMINGWOOD, BOOK V

C. Greenwood

A Beginning

I'm not yet used to the sound of waves crashing against the rocky beach. We've only been on the coast for a day, and everything still seems foreign, so far from Dimmingwood. Sand and pebbles cover the ground where there should be green grass, and there are few trees, just miles of water on the horizon. The breeze is briny instead of smelling like pine and earth. The only birdsongs are the cries of gulls, but they're mostly silent now that the sun has gone down.

There's a full moon out, and combined with a sprinkling of stars overhead, it gives enough light for me to see my footprints leading from camp, where my companions are sleeping. But I don't want their company tonight. I've traveled far these past months, and with farther still to go, I need time alone to stop and think about where I've been...

Chapter One

As I sloshed my way out of the cool stream, I felt cleaner than I had in weeks. Sixteen days on the road with Terrac and Hadrian had not allowed me much private time for luxuries like bathing. So as I waded ashore and wrung the water from my long silver hair, it was a relief to draw a deep breath and find I now smelled like nothing worse than creek water and moss.

Clambering up a nearby boulder, I lay out on the warm rock to dry in the sun. It was early morning, and there wasn't a soul around to break the stillness. My traveling companions back at camp probably weren't even awake yet.

We were all growing spoiled on this journey, I reflected, squinting up at the puffy clouds scuttling across the bright sky. We were away from home, away from the usual responsibilities. After battling the Skeltai savages from across the border and winning, I had a whole year of freedom ahead of me now, a chance to travel and see how people lived beyond my home province of Ellesus. I tried not to think of what would happen when my time was up and I had to return to the Praetor's service.

A soft breeze stirred through the clearing, raising goose pimples on my bare skin. Even though I was still damp, I scrambled down from my perch to drag my warm clothes off the shrub where I'd left them hanging. Despite how far I'd come from Dimmingwood, I still wore my customary forest costume of tunic, leggings, and leather jerkin with deerskin boots. I continued to keep a dagger tucked down one boot and a pair of smaller knives up my sleeves.

I had just finished dressing and was tucking all those knives into place when a sharp cracking sound, like the snap of a stick, broke the stillness of the clearing.

Habit made me drop immediately into a crouch. I scanned the shady grove surrounding the stream, but all was still. There was no sign of any threat, yet I had the uncomfortable feeling of being watched by unseen eyes.

"Terrac?" I called into the trees. "Hadrian?"

No answer.

I strained outward with my magic sense, trying to pick up the presence of an intruder. Of course I felt nothing. I had felt that same empty nothingness ever since my magic was burned out during my recent escape from the Skeltai shaman of the Black Forest. But still I reached for the magic, and still I felt surprise and regret when my grasping came up empty.

I shook my head. I was getting paranoid lately. This wasn't the first time I had felt I was being watched only to discover there was no one there. More than likely, the noise was only made by a wild animal hiding in the shadows. It had more cause to fear me than I it.

I went to retrieve my belt from the shrub. And felt the breeze of something whistling past my cheek to imbed itself with a thud in the trunk of the tree beside me.

It was an arrow.

If I hadn't turned when I did, it would not have missed me. Or maybe it hadn't missed me anyway. A burning, stinging sensation crept up the hollow, fleshy place between my neck and shoulder, and wet blood trickled down my skin.

There was no time to think. Dropping to the ground and rolling behind a nearby tree stump, I tried to get my bearings, tried to figure out what direction the shot had come from. Was it from the tree line directly before me? Cautiously I peered over the stump, and my hand, midway through the motion of drawing one of my throwing knives, froze.

I could see him there, a tall, black-cloaked figure framed by the trees. His hood was back, exposing the gaunt face of a young man not much older than I. His flinty gaze returned my stare for only a second. But during that time, I was struck by a powerful sense of recognition. It was impossible, but I knew him. And it was that knowing that held me immobile.

He visibly hesitated and backed into the shadows before turning to run. I imagined I caught a brief glimpse of the longbow in his hands, and then all I could see was his cloak billowing behind as he disappeared into the trees.

I was too dazed to give chase. For the space of a few heartbeats, I struggled to make sense of what I'd seen, feeling that I had met an apparition from the depths of memory. Then the throbbing of my wound drew my urgent attention. The arrow had barely grazed me, but it must have nicked an artery because an alarming amount of blood was soaking through my tunic.

I ripped off my sleeve and used it to try to slow the bleeding, but fresh blood continued seeping through. Running back to camp pumping out more blood with every step was the last thing I should do, but I didn't have any choice. I needed help, and I would get none here. My attacker could return at any time to finish what he had started. I could not guess what had driven him away.

So I abandoned the unprotected clearing and lost myself in the trees, pushing on in the opposite direction from that my attacker had taken. The wound throbbing and my head feeling strangely light, each step was an effort. Roots rose to trip me, and sharp branches scratched at my face and exposed skin as my vision grew too blurred to avoid them. The morning sunlight faded, and the world grew dark before my eyes, but I couldn't stop to rest. I pressed on, trusting that some part of me knew which direction to go.

Bleeding and confused, I finally stumbled into camp.

Terrac was still sleeping in his blankets, but the priest, Hadrian, was awake and cooking breakfast. He stared as I burst from the thicket. I tried to speak but only managed

5

to mumble something incoherent before collapsing at his feet.

* * *

"We should go after him," Terrac urged, pacing up and down.

Hadrian didn't look up from the bandage he was applying to my throbbing shoulder as he said, "He'll be long gone by now. Anyway, until we know whether this person is working alone or has evil companions lurking nearby, the worst possible thing we could do is split up."

"So we pretend nothing happened and just wait around for him to come back and take another shot at Ilan?"

It warmed me to hear the concern in Terrac's voice, but I wished he would sit still. I had only returned to consciousness a few minutes ago, and his rapid movement to and fro was making me dizzy again.

"Will you stop flapping and come to rest?" I asked. But I made my tone softer than my words, because I had seen the fear in his eyes when he thought I was lost to him.

As Hadrian pulled my bandage tight, I added through gritted teeth, "Whoever or whatever tried to kill me is long out of our reach by now, and I don't think he'll be coming back any time soon."

"What do you mean, 'whatever' it was?" Hadrian asked. "Is there some reason to suppose he was more or less than human?"

I hesitated, remembering the flinty eyes in the hauntingly familiar face. "Maybe. I don't know." I could not bring myself to voice what I really thought, that I had seen a ghost from my past.

Hadrian said, "Then we will treat this as a random attack by some roadside brigand. Doubtless he thought he could snatch your purse and escape unseen, but you caught him in the act and startled him into violence. These highway thieves are cowards at heart. They don't look for a fight, only easy prey."

At the irony of his words—for not long ago we had been simple brigands ourselves—I exchanged a glance with Terrac. Or tried to, but he seemed distracted, and I couldn't catch his eye.

"You two can believe this was some random encounter if you want," Terrac said. "But I do not. I am going back to the stream to have a look around. Maybe this dangerous stranger will have left something behind, some clue to his identity or his intention."

Before Hadrian or I could protest, he grabbed his sword and stomped off into the trees, calling, "I won't be gone long."

"That boy has more courage than sense," Hadrian muttered.

I said nothing as he finished his work on my injured shoulder and began packing away his healing supplies. I couldn't disagree with Terrac. I too knew there was nothing random about what had happened out there. That cloaked man had been out to kill me. There wasn't a doubt in my mind about it.

Giving in to the nagging dizziness, I lay down across the clean blanket Hadrian had spread for me and closed my eyes against the glare of the rising sun. The memory of my attacker's unearthly face played across my eyelids, the last thing I saw as I drifted into a shallow sleep.

* * *

It wasn't until midmorning that I stirred again. Something had awakened me. A soft rustling from the near trees. I blinked up at the pale sky and tried to think why I was resting at this hour. The sun was high above, and the morning's chill had left the ground. All seemed peaceful.

The gentle scratching noises of quill on parchment fell upon my ears, and I was vaguely aware of Hadrian's shadow over me. He scribbled away inside the pages of a book balanced across his knees while simultaneously keeping watch over my slumber. Why should I require his watching?

Sudden awareness of the burning sensation in the hollow between my neck and shoulder brought the memories back in a rush. An arrow piercing my flesh. An unknown menace, whose deadly intent could not match the chilling familiarity of his eyes.

There came another rustle from the trees, accompanied this time by a soft footfall. I bolted upright, instinctively reaching up my sleeve for a knife. But I relaxed when I saw it was only Terrac returning to the camp. And he did not come empty-handed but carried the two halves of a shattered arrow.

"I found no sign in the woods of the villain," he said. "I searched for more than an hour, but he left as little trace as a ghost. When I realized he had covered his trail, I went back to the river. There, at least, he was careless enough to leave behind physical evidence."

He dropped the broken arrow pieces at my feet

Hadrian set aside his ink-stained quill and his book, saying, "There's no mystery in the would-be killer's easy disappearance. A forest thief knows how to cover his trail. You two should know that. Luckily, we are too near our destination to be likely targets of that villain again. I doubt we'll see more of him."

I stopped listening, my eyes drifting to the remnants of the arrow that had so nearly taken my life. It was a fascinating object, not merely because there were dried flecks of my blood spattered across the tip but because there seemed to be some strange, invisible quality surrounding it.

Magic? Surely not. I stretched out my consciousness, seeking to touch the mysterious essence that lingered like a scent over the arrow. But my magic was as elusive as the aura of the arrow, leaving me to wonder if I was only imagining it. To my eyes and to the touch of my fingers, the arrow appeared ordinary in every way.

A discussion was taking place over my head.

"I care not how near our destinations lies." Terrac sounded irritated. "We cannot travel now, not until Ilan has a full day to recuperate."

He rested his hand on my shoulder, maybe out of sympathy or possibly as a silent nudge for my agreement. Either way, it was my injured shoulder and I flinched at his clumsy touch.

"There's no need for this fuss," I told both men. It's my shoulder that's taken a scratch, not my leg. I'm as fit to travel as either of you."

Terrac looked like he wanted to argue. Ever since our relationship had taken its recent turn from the friendly to the tentatively romantic, his attitude toward me had changed. He could be at once overbearing and annoyingly protective.

I cut him off before he could begin. "No arguments. We've wasted enough of the daylight. If our next campsite is as close as Hadrian seems to think, I'd like to reach it before nightfall."

That settled them, and within the hour we broke camp.

* * *

I had thought I could be at home in any woods, but the forested hills of Cros were nothing like what I was accustomed to. The terrain here was increasingly uneven. We always seemed to be climbing sharply upward or plunging down into valleys. The ground was rough, our path littered with rocks and lined with boulders. The grass was thin and sprouted only in occasional tufts between rocks. The spindly trees with leaves sparse on their branches were so different from the lush green canopy of Dimmingwood that it seemed faintly wrong to call them trees at all. Here was no pleasant scent of pine or elder. Even the songs of the local birds were foreign to my ear.

We did not break for our afternoon meal but ate as we walked to make up the lost hours of the morning. I was filled with nervous energy anyway and would not have rested easily. My eyes were constantly on the watch for a dark form moving among the shadows or for the end of a black cloak disappearing behind a tree. But I saw nothing suspicious. I had only the pain in my shoulder and the broken arrow carried inside my traveling pack to prove my encounter with the would-be killer had ever occurred at all.

The afternoon passed and the shadows of the trees had begun to lengthen when the path our party followed took us abruptly out of the wood. We were on open, sloping ground, and my aching feet detected that our path had turned completely to gravel. The steep hills had become small mountains.

I scrambled to catch up to Hadrian, who always seemed to be many yards ahead of Terrac and me despite possessing more years than the both of us combined.

"How much farther have we to go before we reach this camp of yours?" I asked. "Another hour or two and it will be dusk."

For answer, Hadrian climbed a pinnacle of rock and, when I joined him, pointed out over the cliff's edge. Here the world dropped away suddenly into empty air. But across this open space was another rocky peak where jagged cliffs rose opposite ours. There was a valley far below where a wild river rushed freely between high walls of stone.

But my attention wasn't on the canyon. I was looking at the cluster of huts clinging, as if by magic, to the sheer face of the far cliff. These houses were connected to one another by a series of platforms and roped bridges, but how any of them kept their precarious purchase against the rock was impossible to guess. Across the distance, I could see tiny dots that were people moving among the houses and bridges, apparently not the least concerned by the dangerous drop to white river far below them.

"Behold the largest known settlement of magickers anywhere in the provinces," Hadrian said. "This is Swift-on-the-Mountain. Or Swiftsfell, to the locals."

Terrac joined us at the rock's edge. "Swiftsfell? How is it I have never heard the name, when I spent most of my childhood in this province?"

I had nearly forgotten that Cros was Terrac's province of birth, the place where his parents had died and he had first embarked on his journey toward Whitestone Abbey, Dimmingwood, and, ultimately, to me.

"Swiftsfell prefers to avoid attention from the outside world," Hadrian said. "Those lacking magical abilities are typically forbidden entry. This community is a refuge for magickers driven from less hospitable places, where their power is forbidden by law."

Terrac looked uncomfortable, and I guessed he was thinking of how the Praetor had once attempted to cleanse our province of magickers. We rarely spoke of my abilities, but I had the sense he was not altogether sorry my talent had been burnt out of me. Magic made him uneasy.

He said, "If magickless outsiders are discouraged from stopping here, why have we come? It's well enough for the two of you, but I don't have your powers."

"No one says you cannot enter," Hadrian answered. "Only that it will not be by invitation. Even Ilan and I may be looked on with suspicion, as strangers. But if my book of magical races and histories is to be completed, we must find a way to gain the trust of these people." He thumped the thick tome carried inside his travelers pack. "Anyway, we have a dual purpose for this visit. I have information from my sources suggesting Ilan may find Swiftsfell very much of interest."

He looked at me. "I believe this is the magicker settlement you were bound for ten years ago when you set out for Cros."

It was a startling revelation. I thought back to the fateful day Master Borlan had set me atop a peddler's wagon and given the old man instructions to deliver me to a place in Cros where I could live among others of my kind. A place where I would be safe from the soldiers who had killed my parents. But I never reached that mysterious destination thanks to the intervention of a band of forest brigands in Dimmingwood.

I looked over the rooftops of Swiftsfell. Was this really the home that would have awaited me had I finished that long-ago journey? Would this community of magickers have taken me in?

Compelled to learn more of this place and its inhabitants, I had only one question for Hadrian. "How do we get in?"

* * *

"A good question," said Terrac. "It will take us days to make our way down into the canyon and cross the river and even longer to scale the cliff on the other side."

"Perhaps not." Hadrian was mysterious.

He led us down the sharp incline by way of a slippery path that was so rough I was not sure it actually *was* a path at all. It looked as likely to have been carved by wind and weather as by the hand of man.

All the while we descended, Hadrian seemed to be looking for something. We had not gone far when he stopped us. We were on a narrow ledge, just wide enough for the three of us, with a sharp drop-off overlooking the valley below.

"It should be about here," the priest muttered under his breath, and he began exploring the face of the rock, scrubbing away dried clay and moss and scattering pebbles.

"What should be here?" I asked. "What are we supposed to be looking for?"

"There ought to be some sort of symbols or inscription etched into the rock. According to the description from my sources, it must be close."

Terrac caught my eye, and I shrugged. If the priest was determined to be cryptic, it might be faster to help him instead of dragging the facts from him piece by piece. I joined the search, and Terrac followed suit.

"Is this it?" I asked a moment later, glimpsing some foreign writing carved into the stone at eye level. I peeled away the dead moss that had overgrown it until the entire inscription was revealed.

Hadrian came to my side, and together we surveyed the strange writing.

"It is the old tongue," he explained. "You do not see this anymore outside scholarly writings."

"But you can read it?"

"I would not be much of a cleric if I couldn't decipher Old Writ."

As he began to read the ancient words aloud, a chill crept over me.

Chapter Two

A sudden gust of wind came whistling down the canyon. When it hit us, its cold teeth bit through my clothing. As the gust grew stronger, it snatched up Hadrian's words and carried them away.

As thunder rumbled overhead, Terrac touched my arm and pointed skyward. A collection of dark clouds was swiftly forming, roiling directly overhead, while the sky in all other directions remained clear. It was an unnatural sight.

"Are you doing this?" I asked Hadrian over the rising howl of the wind. "I didn't know you had weather abilities."

He finished his incantation and shouted back, "It is no skill of mine. Whoever engraved this spell endowed it with great power."

I raised my eyebrows. "I thought you didn't approve of spells and incantations. You always said they smacked of dark magery."

He put his head closer so I could hear him over the roaring gale. "I do not like any source of magic that is not naturally born. But I trust the goodwill of whoever created this spell."

The intensity of the storm was growing. The wind tossed my hair into my face and ripped at my clothes. Hadrian motioned for me and Terrac to join him in planting our backs against the rock and bracing ourselves against the strength of the gale. Raindrops began to patter down around us.

The priest pointed out over the canyon, toward the distant village on the far cliff. "Look for the void in the rain!"

I wasn't sure I had heard him correctly, but I looked anyway. And as soon as I did, I spotted it. Just a short distance away, the rain appeared to collide with empty air and bounce away as though from a solid object. There was nothing there for the drops to hit, only a yawning emptiness spanning between this cliff and the other. But somehow, impossibly, the rain picked out an invisible shape, a long and narrow stretch where the water spattered and formed pools and finally ran off in little streams.

The others saw it too, and together we approached the invisible bridge.

Terrac would have stepped out first, but I held him back. I did not trust that mysterious surface enough to let him test it. Not when I couldn't see it or whatever supported it.

Hadrian went first. Cautiously he extended his walking-stick in front of him like a blind man, tapping the surface until he was satisfied it was solid enough to hold his weight. He took one step, then two, onto the invisible bridge.

Behind him, I held my breath, waiting for him to fall.

But he did not. Instead he kept going until he was well away from the safety of the ledge and standing, apparently on thin air, above the chasm.

I followed next. It was a strange sensation, walking on a surface I could feel but not see. Looking down between my feet, there was nothing to block my view of the canyon and the rushing river far below.

Whatever materials the bridge was made of, it was dangerously slick with the falling rain. Away from the shelter of the rocks, the wind was unnervingly strong, pushing and pulling at me as if wanting to throw me over the edge. I didn't know whether there were invisible ropes or rails to prevent a fall. My hands found nothing but air to either side.

I was unused to such heights, and the view of the valley so far beneath me was dizzying. I had to stop looking down and focus instead on Hadrian's back just ahead of me, following his every step until, together, we made it to the other side. Moments later, Terrac safely joined us. Only then did I dare to look back.

The wind and rain evaporated as soon as we were on solid ground again, the storm clouds dissipating so suddenly we had only our sodden clothes to prove there had ever been any storm. And without the rain, the bridge too disappeared before my eyes.

We were now on a rocky outcropping at the opposite side of the canyon from where we had started. The only visible way off this ledge was by a short walkway of timber and rope leading to a suspended platform from which branched a series of other walks heading to different parts of the village. At the end of these paths, dozens of small homes clung like the nests of mud-wasps to the sheer face of the rock.

We followed the near walk. Despite its swaying, I felt much safer on the ordinary bridge than on the invisible one we had just crossed.

As we came into what seemed to be the heart of the village, it was clear our arrival, or maybe the storm that made it possible, had not gone unnoticed. Heads poked out of doorways to watch us pass, and the locals crept out of their homes and onto the swinging bridges and suspended platforms. There was something cautious in their movements, as if they were undecided whether to greet us or drive us away.

This was my first close look at the inhabitants of Swiftsfell, and I studied them with interest, remembering what Hadrian had said, that fate had almost delivered me to this place as a child. How different might my life have been if I had grown up here instead of Dimmingwood?

The children looked clean and well fed and as content as any little ones I had ever seen. Among children and adults, I saw a mixture of races and clothing in varied styles that suggested many different provinces. I recognized the rough garb common in the mountainous province of Kersis and the smoother garments and tinkling accessories that might have come from Camdon. I saw too many folk like me, whose pale skin and silver hair denoted a distant Skeltai ancestry. Had all these people fled their home provinces and settled here for the same reason? To be free of persecution toward magickers? I saw more folk who looked like they belonged to my own province than any other, confirming my guess. These people would have sought refuge in Cros during the "cleansing" of Ellesus over a decade ago when the Praetor had attempted to destroy every magicker in the region—and very nearly succeeded.

By the time we reached the end of the walk, many of the villagers had gathered to meet us, their expressions a mixture of curiosity and hostility.

Above their low murmuring, a voice broke through the crowd. "Who are you strangers, and what is it you want?"

The question came from a big fellow, whose height and shock of fiery red hair reminded me briefly of my friend Dradac back home. But there was nothing friendly about the way this man eyed us or the way he held the thick staff in his hand as if it would take very little provocation for him to attack us.

Before we could respond, another voice called out, "Calm yourself, Tomas. Let us give them a chance to speak before we determine them to be our enemies."

The throng parted to reveal the speaker, a stooped old man with a shining, bald head and milky white eyes that stared sightlessly ahead. He rested his hand on the shoulder of a small boy, who steered him expertly through the gathering until he stood before us.

He said, "I apologize for my friend's unenthusiastic greeting. Visitors from the outside are not often seen or encouraged. I am Calder, the elected head of Swiftsfell."

His courteous smile was fixed on a point directly before him.

Hadrian stepped into that empty space. "I greet you, master Calder. I am Hadrian, a priest of the Light, and these are my companions, Ilan of Dimmingwood and Terrac... also of Dimmingwood."

I wondered if his hesitation was because he had almost named Terrac as an Iron Fist in the service of Praetor Tarius but had changed his mind at the last instant. The Praetor of Ellesus would not be a popular man here, and neither would anyone known to be one of his soldiers.

If the village head, Calder, took note of Hadrian's slip, he said nothing of it, instead remarking, "A priest of the Light, you say? I am surprised an Honored One would visit our little village."

Hadrian nodded. "My interest in your community is purely scholarly. I am compiling a history of magic and magical races in the region. It is the first such book of its kind, and if I wish to do it full justice, the work will require me to travel the full breadth of the provinces. But it would not be complete without the inclusion of the largest magicker community in Cros."

Calder looked cautious. "Then you come here seeking information for your book?"

"Only whatever the inhabitants here are willing to share," Hadrian reassured. "I merely wish to interview anyone open to talking with me and answering a few questions. Naturally, I will not record anyone's names or the exact location of this village. I have every respect for the privacy of your community."

Calder's forehead furrowed. "I am not sure this is something I should allow. We in Swiftsfell work hard at secluding ourselves from the outside and, as you have seen with our invisible bridge, have set certain safeguards to maintain our privacy. We would prefer to avoid unwanted attention."

Hadrian asked, "Are such precautions truly necessary? I thought Cros had a more tolerant praetor than ours, one more lenient toward magickers?"

"That is true. But not all persecution comes sanctioned by praetors. There are other sources of danger." The village head looked as if he would say more but then thought better of it. "However, your endeavor sounds like a worthy one, and if any members of the community are willing to take part, it is not for me to forbid it. And I sense that you are not quite a stranger to our kind, are you?"

"I am not," Hadrian agreed. "I was born with the gift of natural magic, as was one of my companions here."

I was glad when he did not single me out or go into detail. The loss of my powers was not a thing I was eager to share with strangers. As it was, this Calder could probably sense the flicker of what had once been in me.

Thankfully, he did not pursue the subject. "I will not deny your party permission to stay in Swiftsfell for a few days. We will need to discuss boundaries for your mission to ensure the safety of our people is not compromised. But this is not the time or place for such a discussion. I invite you and your companions to be guests in my home. Perhaps we may clarify matters over dinner."

I had been following the conversation up to this point, but now I was distracted by a face in the crowd. A petite old woman had stationed herself at the front of the onlookers and was studying me with a strange look of fascination. As if unable to contain herself any longer, she pushed forward now.

"Ada ," she burst out. "Ada, it is you!"

I blinked. The woman was looking directly at me, but I kept silent, half expecting someone else to step forward in answer to her question.

When I did not respond, she came closer until she stood right before me. For a brief moment I thought she was going to reach out and touch me. The dazed look in her eyes, as if she could not believe what she was seeing, was unnerving. Unconsciously, I stepped back from her.

At my motion, the light in her eyes died, the expression of confused hope being replaced by resignation and disappointment.

"Oh," she said dully. "You are not she."

"No," I agreed. "I am Ilan."

She recovered herself briskly. "But you bear a resemblance to her, so I am not a mad old fool for thinking it. Do you know Ada?"

My heart beat a little faster. "That was the name of my mother."

Her eyes lit up. "Then your Ada and mine are one and the same—and how like her you are! It is no wonder I was confused."

Instantly I was intrigued. I had never met any friends of my mother, and it was startling to find one here where I had least expected it.

"You knew my mother?" I asked. "When? What can you tell me about her?"

"It would be better to ask what you can tell me," she countered. "For I have not seen her this past decade."

I swallowed. "I am sorry to tell you she is dead."

The woman's eyes reflected pain. "That I have long known. But I would like to hear of how she died and of the life she lived since I last saw her. And in return, perhaps I can answer your questions as well."

"Ilan," Terrac cut in. "Calder is leading the way."

He was right. The village head and Hadrian were departing together, and if Terrac and I did not hurry, we were in danger of being left behind.

I made up my mind quickly. "You go on with Hadrian, and I will find the both of you later," I said. "I need another moment here."

I could see he was displeased at the separation, but turning back to the old woman, I did not give him the chance to protest.

"Is there someplace we could talk privately?" I asked.

She nodded her silver head. "Of course. Come with me."

* * *

From the outside, the old woman's house was the same as all the others. Again it occurred to me that these cliff homes looked vaguely like mud-wasp nests turned on their sides. The sheer face of the cliff formed their backs, and their outer walls were a mixture of timber and dark clay constructed into tunnellike shapes. Each was stacked directly over the next in connected rows. Swaying rope bridges ran between each cluster of homes, joining them like a great hive.

Inside, my host's home was unlike anything I had ever encountered. Long and narrow, the rooms were like passages, each leading into the next with no central room or entryway to connect them. But that hardly mattered because there were few rooms anyway. She apparently had little need of space, which was as well, because the overall feeling of her house was of a cramped but cozy atmosphere.

"Would you like a drink?" she asked. Without awaiting an answer, she went to the fireplace, a small niche carved out of the inner rock wall, and fetched a kettle from over the low flames.

She moved with surprising ease for a woman of her years, and I mentally adjusted my first impression of her from elderly to a bit past middle-aged. Like myself and many of Swiftsfell's inhabitants, she bore evidence of Skeltai ancestry, and the silverness of her hair combined with the heavy lines of her face made her age difficult to guess.

I took a seat on a bench near the fire. On such a warm day, the proximity of the flames was mildly uncomfortable, but every other surface I might have sat on seemed occupied by baskets and blankets and various kinds of clutter I could not identify. My bench was rickety and roughly put together, like all the other furnishings in the room. The floor was scattered with rushes as a primitive replacement for rugs. The mud-dobbed outer walls were hung with big woven mats, presumably as an extra layer of insulation during the winter months.

It took me a moment to take all this in as my eyes grew accustomed to the dimness of the windowless space. The fireplace cast a little light around the room, but a cooler source of illumination was the series of lamps resting on tabletops and other surfaces. The bluish color from the lamps made me wonder if they were lit by some means less natural than ordinary flame. This was, after all, a place where magic could be used freely and openly.

My thoughts returned to my host when she passed a warm cup into my hand. The scent of the steaming *skeil* was reassuring. The drink, at least, was familiar.

"Now," she said, seating herself on a nearby stool. "Let us introduce ourselves properly. My name is Myria. I did not catch yours."

It seemed strange to be introducing ourselves so formally, after our excited initial meeting. But perhaps neither of us knew quite how to act toward the other.

"Ilan of Dimmingwood. That's the forest that covers half the province of Ellesus."

"And what is it that brings you to Swiftsfell, Ilan of Dimmingwood?"

"Nothing more than you already know," I said, trying to contain my impatience. On the way to her home, I had tried to ask her what she knew about my mother, but this Myria seemed suddenly distracted. Still, I forced myself to be polite. Demanding answers would get me nowhere.

So I explained, "As my friend Hadrian was telling the head of your village, he is compiling a book. It is a history of magic and a study of magically gifted races."

She appeared dissatisfied with my explanation. "I did not ask for your friends' motives in coming here but yours. I believe your province is a fair distance from the mountains of Cros. Something must have compelled you to make the journey."

I hesitated, but there seemed no danger in speaking frankly to this stranger. We were not back home, where I had to cloak certain aspects of my past. "I had reasons for

27

wanting to put my province behind me. I was recently pressed into the service of a man I count my enemy. I cannot escape my duties indefinitely for, when a year has passed, I've promised to return. But until then, I accompany the wandering priest on his travels. And where I go, Terrac goes."

"Because he is in love with you?"

"Because the Praetor of our province does not trust me to keep my word. He sent Terrac to ensure that I do not forget my promises."

I didn't tell her how that troubled me. I liked to think that I, and not the Praetor, owned the greater part of Terrac's loyalty, but the truth was that I had never really pressed him to choose between us.

Myria's thoughts followed a different direction than mine. "So you travel where your priest friend does. You did not come to Swiftsfell on your own account?"

"Why should I do that?"

She lifted a silver eyebrow. "When I realized whose kin you were, I thought you might have visited in search of your past. Looking for your mother's people, perhaps."

At last we were heading in the right direction. I said, "I do not remember my mother ever speaking of friends or family from her past. I had no cause to suppose any existed, let alone that they should be found in Swiftsfell. I'm sorry to say she did not mention you."

"I understand." Refilling my drink, she changed the subject. "And how did you lose your magical abilities?"

I started, nearly sloshing my hot beverage onto my hand. "How did you—"

But then I realized I shouldn't be surprised. Just as I used to feel the presence or absence of magic in others, so must other magickers sense it in me. To this woman, the power that had recently abandoned me was probably as evident as smoke curling from a newly snuffed candle.

"My magic was burned out."

It sounded abrupt, but I found myself unexpectedly sensitive on the subject. Her question felt awkwardly personal. If I were missing an arm, would she be tactless enough ask how I had lost that?

If she noticed my reaction, her expression was unapologetic. "Many a young, untrained magicker has overextended herself and destroyed her skill beyond hope of healing."

"I was not untrained. Hadrian has mentored me these past three years. I was simply in a position where I had to make a choice. Push my magic past safe limits or allow a friend to die. I took the risk, and I don't regret it."

It was true. If I hadn't sacrificed my magic to defend Terrac against a Skeltai shaman, he would be dead now. His life was worth the cost.

"I am glad you were loyal to your friend," said Myria. "But a lifetime separated from your natural gift is a high price to pay."

I feigned a casualness I did not feel. "What's done is done. I would rather not dwell on it."

"It may be that you are right." Myria tilted her silver head to one side and tapped a slender finger against her chin thoughtfully. "But sometimes what we think is done is not really over at all."

She hesitated, then appeared to come to a sudden decision. "Come with me, young Ilan. There's something I'd like to show you. It's a test, of sorts."

I was baffled. "What kind of a test?"

Instead of answering, she vacated her seat by the fire and gestured me to follow as she crossed the room to draw back a thin curtain. The chamber beyond was scarcely worthy of the name. It was more of an alcove, with just space enough for a clothes chest and a hammock slung along the wall.

She beckoned me to a shelf that held an assortment of mismatched odds and ends. Broken shells, bits of jewelry, framed miniatures, and a carved wooden box of the kind often used to hold small mementoes.

She lifted the memento box down from the shelf. It was small, not much bigger than the hand that held it, but she handled it carefully as though its contents were great.

Her eyes met mine over the box. "What I am about to show you must be our secret. For although no one in Swiftsfell would steal it from me, there are others outside the village who would give much to possess what I hold."

"Others?" My mind went to the general sense of wariness that seemed to hang over Swiftsfell and its inhabitants.

She followed my thoughts. "We are not easy with our Drejian neighbors in the near mountains. They have no liking for us, and neither does the dragon, Micanthria, whom they harbor."

She shrugged slender shoulders. "But it is no matter, for I trust you to keep my treasure secret."

"Treasure?"

"Perhaps I had better call it a family heirloom, for it was passed down from my mother, who discovered it entirely by accident."

Without further explanation, she flipped the box lid back on its hinge to reveal its mysterious contents.

I half expected to find some sort of jewel twinkling up at me, but instead I was met with the sight of a plain, flat rock smaller than my palm resting atop a folded kerchief. The stone was flat and dark gray, like a piece of shale, but there was an iridescent sheen to the smooth surface, and it shimmered in the lamplight. The piece was meant to be worn as an ornament, and a silver chain snaked through a hole that had been punched in its center.

"How very unusual," I said, trying to look suitably impressed. It was a pretty enough ornament, for someone who couldn't afford better, but hardly looked worthy of the term 'treasure.'

Myria fingered the item. "I see you do not know what you behold. This is no ordinary ornament but the scale of a dragon."

My blank expression must have disappointed her because she added. "As you have been instructed in the ways of magic by your priest friend, I am sure you understand that dragon teeth, claws, and scales are a few of the many objects which possess magical properties. Such objects are sometimes used to augment a magicker's natural powers."

I understood nothing of the kind. It was exactly the sort of subject Hadrian would have avoided discussing with me. He detested any attempt to create or capture magic where it did not formerly exist. It sounded as though this dragon scale skirted dangerously close to that line.

Myria continued, "A dragon's scale is one of the most coveted augmenters among magickers. Even a magickless person could use it if he were skilled in the unnatural art of magery. But it is not the greed of mages that concerns me."

"The Drejians you spoke of?" I guessed.

"Just so. It is risky to possess such an object now that Drejians have settled into these parts. If they learned of the augmenter, they might wish to possess it. That is why I am making it a gift to you. You may take it away when you leave, for I will rest easier to think of it being carried far from their reach."

I hesitated, wondering what Hadrian would say to my possessing an augmenter. I could not imagine he would approve. But if it was a favor to this woman…

Unaware of my internal struggle, Myria lifted the dragon scale from its box and pressed it into my palm, closing my fingers around it.

All my doubts evaporated instantly. Something unexpected flickered inside me at the cool touch of the augmenter, something I had not felt in far too long.

Magic.

Chapter Three

Instinctively, I grasped the magic as a drowning person might clutch at a rope, with the wild fear that it might be snatched away again at any moment. It was a strange sensation, filtering power through the augmenter instead of drawing it directly from the source. It felt muffled, less immediate. But compared to going without, it was good, like regaining a lost sense. One I hadn't known I missed so badly until it was restored.

Filled with magic, I was aware of Myria at my side in a way I hadn't been previously. Before, I had seen and heard her. But now I could vaguely pick up her emotions. Her face was placid, but inside she was... hopeful. Sad. Pleased. A curious mixture of emotions.

I felt the presence of other people too, Myria's neighbors moving about in their cottages. I stretched my senses farther and found Terrac and Hadrian somewhere in the distance. I couldn't read their minds, of course, or tell what they were doing. But their emotions were quiet, indicating they were safe and content.

After spending the past weeks closed off from such knowledge, this was a sudden wealth of awareness.

Myria had been watching me, noting my reactions. "You rely a great deal on empathy, don't you?"

I shrugged. "Tracking people's movements and feeling out their moods has always come naturally to me."

"It is good to have an area of strength. Your mother had one too. But I hope you do not practice this one to the exclusion of others."

"I don't think of it as exclusion. It's something I fall back on unconsciously."

"But your mentor, the priest, has taught you more than this?"

"We used to practice and exercise many skills before I lost my powers," I said. "Most of them mental or emotional. Why? What was my mother's special ability?"

She glanced around. "It is not something I could safely show you indoors. Come with me."

I followed her outside. Evening had fallen, and the last light of day was fading on the horizon. Peering over the railed walkway, I could barely see through the gathering gloom to make out the white river flowing far below us.

Joining me at the rail, Myria stretched out a hand toward the river, and a streak of blue light shot from her fingertips to blaze a trail through the shadows.

I lifted my eyebrows. "I can see why you didn't want to do that indoors."

"My aim is not always reliable," she admitted ruefully. "But your mother's was better."

"I know. I've seen her summon lightning like that." A memory flashed through my head of Mama holding off the Praetor's soldiers with the blue fire crackling from her fingertips. It was the last thing she ever did.

I shoved the memory aside and asked, "Could you show me how to do it?"

"Of course. And after you have mastered the skill, you will learn to modify it for other purposes. The same technique can be used in forming a ball of light to illumine the darkness or in creating a spark to light a campfire. You will find it useful for many purposes."

A niggling concern tugged at me. "Hadrian never taught me things like this. Maybe it was beyond his abilities, or perhaps he did not think they were necessary. Either way, I am reluctant to proceed behind his back. He would likely not approve of the augmenter either."

"You want to consult him?" she asked.

"I am not going to ask for his permission. But I value his guidance and want to hear his thoughts on this."

The rash young thief who used to be me would have shuddered at such a comment. But nowadays I was learning not to take my friends for granted. I didn't have many left.

She nodded. "Then perhaps we will return to this another time."

I agreed. "Maybe now would be a good time for you to answer those questions I asked earlier. About my mother?"

At the change in topic, I sensed a wave of sadness settle over Myria. "You look a great deal like Ada."

"You said as much before. You also said that you were aware of her death. Can I ask how the news reached you?"

"Ada and I shared a special bond. I felt it severed in the moment when her life was extinguished, even though there was a long distance between us. Later, I tried to discover the details of her death, but no one could tell me."

As she spoke, a gradual awareness came to me. Since first we met, I had sensed a connection to this silver-haired woman, one not felt in the presence of another person in a long time. I tried to recall the last occasion when I had experienced this. It was in the presence of the Praetor. The man was my uncle, though he did not know it.

That was when I realized the truth.

"You and I share the same blood," I blurted out to Myria. "That is why there is this link between us. My mother was not your friend but your kinswoman."

"She was my daughter," Myria said, correcting me.

I squeezed my eyes shut and leaned back against the rail, knees weak, legs suddenly inadequate. Our previous conversations took on new light as I thought of the miniatures lined up on Myria's shelf, of a particular portrait I had noticed, a rough sketch of a silver-haired girl. It had looked familiar, and now I knew why. It was a youthful version of my mother.

I tried to wrap my mind around this new revelation. "So you are…"

"Your grandmother," she supplied. "But you do not have to call me that. Not when we know one another so little."

Blinking, I took a slow breath. "And do I have any other family I should know about?"

"None surviving. That is why it was such a blow when I became aware of Ada's death."

Her eyes misted with unshed tears, and I realized how hard it was for her to speak casually of her loss.

I swallowed. It was strange that a person I had only just met shared a grief with me that even my closest friends could not know. Strange but comforting.

I made a decision. "If you would like, I could tell you how she died."

* * *

Myria and I stayed up late into the night. I told her the story of how my parents had been killed all those years ago and of my own fate after. But we shared more than sorrow because there were good stories to be told too. Myria described my mother in her childhood and told me she had last seen her when she was little older than I was now. She had married a man from Ellesus, my father, and settled in that province, never to see her own mother again. My existence had never even been guessed at until now.

I spent that night sleeping on a cot in the small cottage, thinking as I drifted to sleep how much had changed in the past day. Thanks to the dragon scale on its chain now nestling in the hollow of my throat, I could access magic again. It wasn't like before, when the magic had come directly to me. But in time I would surely get used to filtering it through the augmenter. And I had found my family, or what was left of it. Mama had no brothers or sisters, and my grandfather was long deceased. But at least there was Myria. She was a stranger to me, but with the link of our common blood, our bond could only grow.

I awoke in the morning to find Terrac had come for me. He and Hadrian had passed the night as guests of Calder, but Terrac had been worried when I failed to join them.

I reintroduced him to Myria—I wasn't ready to call her "Grandmother" yet—and she made us both a good breakfast. Then although I was reluctant to leave so soon, with Myria's reassurance we would talk more later, I let Terrac lead me away.

Calder's home was at the far side of the village, but I didn't mind the distance. I was already growing used to the heights that had made me dizzy yesterday. Besides, it was a pleasant, sunny morning, and my heart was light.

Terrac's, I quickly realized, was not.

Wearing the augmenter, I was aware of his mood in a way I had not been in some weeks. As we walked hand in hand across the suspended walkways, I wondered what was troubling him. Why did his mood feel so sour? Maybe I should ask, but I did not want any unpleasantness leeching away my good humor.

Instead, I told him of my newfound connection to Myria and was relieved when he seemed pleased for me.

Calder's house was bigger than Myria's but crowded because all his children and grandchildren lived packed under one roof with him. It was a convenient arrangement because the old man never lacked an affectionate grandson or granddaughter to lead him around by the hand. But the noise of so many voices and the commotion of so many small bodies was hectic. I was relieved when we left them behind and shut ourselves into a separate room that seemed something like a study.

Hadrian and Calder greeted us here, Hadrian barely looking up from the books and scrolls Calder was shoving at him.

"It is a continual regret to me that I am no longer able to read them," the blind man was saying. "But I am pleased you, at least, may make some use of them."

"What is this?" I asked, pointing to an intriguing-looking parchment on the table before the two men.

Hadrian was painstakingly copying the sketch into his book. "That is a map of the Arxus Mountains, not far from us."

"And they are important?" I wondered.

"They matter to us in Swiftsfell," Calder put in, "because the Drejians have made their home on this side of the range."

Drejians. Myria had mentioned them in our conversation last night. "Those are the people you are at war with?"

"There is no war," Calder corrected. "Not really. The Drejians merely plague us and other neighboring communities, demanding tribute in exchange for leaving us in peace."

Terrac interrupted. "But surely they have no authority to make such demands. Your province is governed by a praetor, the same as ours. What does he say to the Drejian threats against his people?"

Calder shrugged. "The local praetor does nothing, and he never will. As long as the dragon people do not trouble the cities, he leaves the villages bordering the desert and mountains to fend for themselves."

"And do you pay the tribute?" I asked.

"So we have in the past." Calder looked troubled. "But you come to us at a dangerous time. The Drejians have a ridiculous impression that we here in Swiftsfell have amassed some sort of hidden wealth. You have seen how simply we live here. But they are determined to believe we are sitting on secret piles of gold, which we withhold from them out of greed. Because of this, their demands have grown increasingly more unreasonable until at last we find ourselves unable to meet them. We have missed the time for our payment and have nothing left to give. This is why you find us in a state of wariness and why you would be well advised not to remain with us long. There is no sense in your becoming caught up in whatever is to come."

"Then you fear a consequence, an attack of some sort?" asked Hadrian.

Calder said, "The Drejians are a fierce and violent people, and they have the dragon, Micanthria, on their side. I do not know what they might resort to if their threats go unanswered. I fear for the safety of this village."

"What sort of precautions have you taken?" I asked.

"We have a magical web extended around our perimeters and would be instantly aware of anyone approaching or attempting to enter Swiftsfell. This same defense warned us of your coming."

"You made no efforts to stop us," Terrac pointed out.

"I sensed no ill purpose in your party and was intrigued to see what brought you to our village.

"And now that we are here," I said, "we would like to offer our help."

"We would?" Terrac repeated incredulously.

Calder looked startled, Hadrian merely thoughtful.

"Our enemies are not the sort you would wish to make your own," Calder cautioned.

I thought of Myria, my grandmother, and knew I already had a tie to this place and its inhabitants that could not be undone. I said, "I would like to learn more about these Drejian neighbors of yours."

Calder smiled, as if amused by my refusal to be warned. "Very well, my young friend. I may have something to help you find the information you seek."

His hands moved among the dusty stacks of books on the table. Even deprived of his sight, he seemed able to tell the books apart by their positioning and the feel of their covers. After a brief exploration, he withdrew one volume from a stack and offered it to me.

"This is a collection of Drejian tales and mythology and, if memory serves, contains some true historical accounts. Its study may bring you a clearer understanding of the Drejian culture. Because knowing your enemy is half the battle."

* * *

I spent all morning and afternoon at the house. I studied the book from Calder, and for a while I listened to Hadrian interviewing the village head. Then when Terrac gave in to the pleading of Calder's small grandchildren, I watched him play games with them. It was amusing to see because he usually lost.

I declined invitations to stay for dinner because I had spent too much of the day away from Myria already. I should be using every opportunity to get to know her better.

When I stepped out the door and started toward my grandmother's cottage, I discovered the weather was no longer as pleasant as it had been in the morning. The sky was overcast, and the wind sweeping down the canyon carried the chill of evening.

Reminded of the storm during yesterday's crossing of the invisible bridge, I looked across the divide to the cliff on the far side. And froze, midstride.

A figure stood there at the edge of the cliff. He was only a dark, indistinct blur in the distance, his cloak swirling around him in the wind. But I did not need to see his features, the face that had been so hauntingly familiar when he had tried to kill me that day by the river.

Chapter Four

My enemy was motionless now, but I could feel his eyes on me, and with the help of my new augmenter I sensed his menacing presence in a way I could not before. The half-healed wound between my neck and shoulder smarted at the memory of his arrow's graze. We stood like that, staring at one another across the long gap, until a footfall from behind made me jump.

But it was only Terrac.

"What's wrong? What are we looking at?" he asked, joining me at the rail of the walkway.

I nodded toward the stranger across the divide. "It's the one who tried to kill me the other day. He's found us here."

Terrac followed my gaze, but even as I spoke my would-be assassin stepped back from the rock's edge, disappearing from view.

"He was there," I insisted at Terrac's questioning look. "I think he is looking for some way to cross to this side."

"Let him look. He'll never find the bridge. And even if he did, I wouldn't let him get to you."

He put a comforting arm around me. But I still could not shake the dread the sight of that dangerous stranger inspired in me. Suddenly, Swiftsfell no longer felt like such a safe place.

"You're shivering." Terrac removed his coat and slipped it around my shoulders. I did not tell him it wasn't the cold wind that made me shudder.

"I'm fine. Anyway, I had better get back to Myria. She will wonder why I've been gone so long."

"I'm beginning to think you prefer the company of Myria, Hadrian, and even that musty old Calder to mine."

He was teasing, but I sensed discontent behind his words. He had not been himself since our arrival here. Was it the proximity of so many magickers? He was used to Hadrian and me, but maybe he did not trust these villagers. With suspicion of magickers so prevalent, maybe it would be strange if he *was* comfortable in this community.

I try to reassure him with jokes as we walked back to Myria's cottage. But when he briefly kissed me goodnight and left me at the door, I was still aware of an unspoken awkwardness between us.

Again I looked across the canyon to the far side, but the menacing stranger remained hidden from sight. Was he watching me even now?

I shook my head. I would not worry about him. The villagers had that magical "web" Calder spoke of, and it would trigger a warning if an outsider attempted to enter the village stealthily. As long as that remained in place, I had nothing to fear.

Nonetheless, when I went to bed that night, I set up my own web of magic to alert me if anyone besides Myria and I moved around the house. Then I settled down to sleep in my cot before the fire. Temperatures had continued to fall, and the night was cool. Myria had given me a blanket, but I preferred snuggling under Terrac's coat, which I had brought home with me. It smelled like him.

As I turned over, trying to get comfortable, something stiff, with pointed corners, crumpled in the coat's inner pocket. I slipped a hand inside and fished out a folded sheet of parchment. It occurred to me fleetingly that its contents might be private. But surely if they were, Terrac would not have left them for me to find. Besides, before setting out on this journey, we had made a pact not to keep secrets anymore.

Giving in to my curiosity, I unfolded the letter and crept closer to the fire. Under the flickering glow, I made out what seemed to be a brief log of our travels, noting the dates and locations of our various stops. Most of it was devoted to our arrival yesterday in the magicker village.

Numbness sweeping over me, I folded the report and replaced it where I had found it. I wanted to deny what I had seen and silence the dark thoughts racing through my head. But I could not. There was no question that the note was written in Terrac's hand. He had taught me my letters when we were just a pair of younglings, and I knew his familiar script as well as my own. Neither was there any possibility of misinterpretation.

No, it didn't matter how much I wanted to disbelieve. There was no doubt what I had in my possession and just as little doubt for whose eyes it was intended. Terrac was recording our travels, and in particular our encounters with magickers, for the Praetor. His ambition had long been his weakness, and now he was using his relationship with me and even his friendship with Hadrian to make himself invaluable to his master. To the one man who most despised natural magickers and had made it his mission to destroy us. It didn't matter that the Praetor was technically my master too these days, that I was sworn to his service on eventually returning to the province. In my heart, he was still my enemy, the one responsible for the death of my parents.

And Terrac knew this. Yet he would spy for the man, betraying me in the process, knowing I would never approve his actions. His change in mood since our arrival in Swiftsfell made sudden sense now. He knew and I knew that he continued to serve the Praetor, but we had thus far avoided conflicting interests. Swiftsfell would change that.

I shoved Terrac's warm coat off me, letting it drop to the floor, and replaced it with Myria's spare blanket. The wool blanket smelled faintly musty, as if it had been stored a long time in a trunk, but I didn't care. I lay awake for hours, wondering what I should do. I could not allow Terrac to make that report.

* * *

My dreams that night were a jumbled mixture of Terrac, the Praetor, and the mysterious stranger who was tracking me. As I had done a thousand times before, I relived that long-ago night when my parents had been killed. Only as the child version of me fled the burning house and the chaos in the yard, escaping into the safety of the trees, she looked back to see Terrac among the Praetor's soldiers. Terrac watching and approving as they cut down Da and trampled Mama beneath the hooves of their horses.

I woke in a sweat and lay in the shadows beneath the dying glow of the fireplace, trying to calm the pounding of my heart against my ribs. The dream wasn't a true representation of events. Terrac would have been only a child all those years ago and had been nowhere near the place where it happened. Still, it was hard to shake those images from my mind or dispel the feelings that came with them.

When I eventually slipped back into a fitful slumber, I saw the cloaked stranger in my mind's eye. I saw him scaling the far side of the canyon and looking for a way to cross the rushing river.

He was getting closer.

* * *

The next morning, I tried to distract myself from my worries by delving further into the book Calder had loaned me. The Drejian tales and histories within were strange and might have been interesting at another time. But I could not concentrate on them now

Myria told me over breakfast that she would be harvesting hucklefruit in the high field all morning. She asked me to join her, and I agreed, although it was a confusing invitation. I had not seen any place in Swiftsfell that might be worthy of the name "field," and I couldn't see how crops could possibly grow down the face of a cliff.

But Myria smiled mysteriously and assured me I would see for myself in good time. Then she led me away from the breakfast table and into her room, where she opened the trunk at the foot of her hammock.

She said, "If you are going to work alongside the local women, you might as well look as if you belong with us."

She withdrew a colorful costume from the trunk, a dark gold dress with long, split sleeves and matching leggings. After giving me a sturdy pair of thick-soled ankle boots, she clipped a jingling belt of looped silver rings around my waist.

Then she stood back to examine me. Her eyes were misty. "These things were worn by your mother when she was your age. After she left, I never had the heart to throw them out or give them away. But it is right that you should have them now."

For the longest time, the only thing I'd had of my mother's was the brooch she had given me on the night of her death. I wore it often, pinned to my collar. But it had represented my Da's side of the family, the house of

Tarius. This was different because it was hers. I felt closer to her, wearing her clothes.

At the same time, I had never dressed in anything so garish. The skirt impeded my movements and was altogether impractical, but at least I approved of the boots, which were better suited than my own to the rocky terrain.

Myria plaited my silver hair over one shoulder, the way I had noticed many of the Swiftsfell girls wearing theirs, and when she was done I looked remarkably like the portrait of my mother looking down on us from its place on the nearby shelf.

The final touch, as we left the house, was to grab a pair of long sacks to be looped with string over our shoulders. These were for collecting the hucklefruit.

Outside, the cool temperatures from the night before persisted, but at least the wind had died down and the sun was bright.

My grandmother and I joined a handful of other women and children who carried sacks like ours and were heading the same direction. Apprehensively, I watched the others clambering easily up the rope ladders that scaled the rock and led high above the roofs of the village. Despite her years, Myria scrambled after them with ease born of long practice.

I swallowed my doubts and struggled along behind, trying not to look down. I had never scaled anything higher or more complicated than the elder trees back in Dimmingwood, and my feet kept tangling clumsily in the rope webbing.

I was out of breath by the time I reach the end of my climb and pulled myself over the cliff's side and onto solid ground. Here the high field spread before me. Although the name summoned images of waving, golden grass, the field was more like a carefully cultivated garden with row on row of tall green stalks or smaller patches of berries and mushrooms.

Myria explained that the field was tended by the women and children of the village, while the men fished with nets in the river far below. Between the field and river, the people here were able to supply their own food through the year.

"Even in the cold winter months?" I asked.

She explained that the hardier plants could survive in any season, especially with the right help. She motioned me to join her, kneeling amongst a patch of brown-leaved creeping plants. They looked dead or close to it, but when my grandmother spread her hands over them, they revived before my eyes, the withered leaves and stems filling out and turning a lush green.

"This is your gift," I realized. "You help things grow."

She smiled agreement and took my hands in hers. "You try."

She spread my hands, palms down, over the plants and talked me through the mental techniques. But despite my best efforts at following her instructions and drawing the magic through my dragon-scale augmenter, I could not seem to do what she had.

"Some lack the aptitude for it," Myria said. "Do not be discouraged. You are skilled in empathy, and you may have other talents waiting to be discovered. Maybe something like this."

She made a rolling motion with her hand, and suddenly a glowing orb of light appeared, hovering over her palm.

Impressed, I asked, "Why do you make that motion with your hand?"

"The flourish is unnecessary but is how I learned to do it when I was young. Some magickers keep those early habits and find them helpful for remembering the accompanying mental exercises."

"Like a child learning sums by counting on her fingers?"

"Exactly. Would you like to try it?"

I hesitated. I had not found the chance to discuss any of this with Hadrian. Did it matter? I decided it didn't.

With Myria's help, I made several attempts and finally succeeded at summoning a tiny ball of light. It was fainter than hers and disappeared the instant I lost my concentration, but I took it as a victory. Next my grandmother tried to instruct me in summoning lightning, but the best I could manage was a small spark.

Realizing the other harvesters were watching us, the children giggling at my clumsy failures, I gave up and turned my attention to the simpler work of collecting the hucklefruit. It was good to lose myself in such a simple activity. But I could not stop my mind wandering as I worked. I thought of the mysterious enemy I had spotted watching me last night and felt suddenly exposed on the cliff top.

Then my mind moved in a still more troubling direction. What was I going to do about Terrac and my discovery of his secret?

"You should speak to him," said Myria, as she worked at my side.

"What? Speak to who?"

"I may be aging, but I am not blind, granddaughter. Yesterday all was well between you and your young man. But today your thoughts are troubled. I imagine you only came to the field with me in order to avoid him in case he were to come looking for you."

I smothered a flash of irritation, not at her but at myself. "Am I so readable?"

"Only to someone who cares enough to look. Anyway, I think you are done running away from your problem."

"Why is that?"

She smiled. "Because the problem has come to you."

She nodded to where the wall of green stalks ended, and sure enough, Terrac was there.

How had he known where to find me?

He looked so casual as he approached that my anger flared at the sight of him. How could he smile like that when he was lying to me? I made up my mind in a split second and stalked down the row to meet him. Ignoring his greeting, I produced the report I had been carrying with me for just such an occasion and waved it beneath his nose.

"Tell me the meaning of this," I demanded. "I found it in your coat last night."

Recognition flickered in his eyes, and something else. Irritation. "What did you do? Search my pockets?" His tone was cool.

Mine wasn't. "You left it where I could easily find it. It didn't take much looking. Anyway, I'm not the one whose actions need defending. At first I could not believe what I was seeing. I wanted to think there was some better explanation than the obvious."

His jaw set in a stubborn expression I knew all too well. "A better explanation than what? If you have some accusation to make, I deserve to hear what it is."

"Do not insult me by pretending ignorance. You knew what you were doing was wrong, or you would not have attempted to keep it secret. You're spying for the Praetor."

Conscious of the curious attention we were drawing from Myria and the other onlookers, I lowered my voice. "When we get back home, you plan to report the location of this magicker village, even though you know it could endanger Swiftsfell."

His expression became unreadable. "There is nothing secret about this place or the people in it. If the Praetor wanted to learn about them, he could get his information anywhere. And nothing in my report will hurt your grandmother or the other people here. This province is not even under our Praetor's authority."

I shook my head. "Then why lie to me?"

"There was never any lie. You've always known I was sent on this journey to keep an eye on you. To ensure your return and report your activities."

It was true, but my anger was in no way abated. "I didn't realize you would be taking your duties quite so seriously. You have noted our every stop, our every interaction with the locals. You have been using me and Hadrian like a pair of bloodhounds to hunt down magickers."

He winced. "That's an exaggeration. I came on this journey to be with you. But at the end of this year of freedom, you and I both have to return to the province and the Praetor's service. It's only wise to curry favor with him while we have the opportunity. I know you hate that sort of thing, and that is why I plan on handling it for the both of us. You must realize this is only good sense."

"What I realize is that you are as ambitious as you ever were and that you do not hesitate to betray your friends."

"Don't say that. I am acting for the both of us."

"And yet you didn't consult me."

"You mean the way you always consult me?" His voice was heavy with sarcasm. "When was the last time you did that, Ilan? When have you asked my opinion on anything? Ever?"

I hesitated, because he was right.

"It is true," I said. "You and I have very different priorities, and we are both too independent to rely on another's instincts. That is why this was all one big mistake. *We* are a mistake."

He looked bewildered. "What are you saying?"

"That you and I don't have a lot of trust in our history. I was used to the backstabbing old Terrac who was sometimes my friend and sometimes my enemy. I knew how to deal with him. But whatever we are to each other now requires a whole new level of faith, and it is clear we don't have that. We never will."

Surprise and confusion mingled in his expression. "Do not say things like that, Ilan. You are angry now, but tomorrow you will feel differently."

"No, I will not," I said sadly. "Because you and I are done."

They were the hardest words I ever spoke, and I could not look at him while I said them. So I turned fast to walk away.

"Ilan, wait."

I had only gone two steps when he caught my arm, jerking me to a halt, and spun me around.

But whatever he was about to say or do was cut off when sudden screams erupted all around.

Chapter Five

A dark shadow fell over us, blotting out the sunshine, and there was a rushing, whooshing sound. I looked up to see a giant dark blur of glittering scales and gaping jaws descending over the field.

I had never seen anything like this and did not know what I was looking at until one of the pickers nearby screamed, "Dragon!"

There was no time to think. The beast swooped low, the wind from its massive, flapping wings stirring a mini hurricane of dust and leaves.

Instinctively, I threw myself to the ground, and Terrac dropped beside me as the monster passed so close over our heads we could almost have touched her. I had a brief impression of burning eyes and flashing white claws, and then Terrac blocked my view, shielding me with his body.

There was a roaring sound and a swift wave of heat, as if we were suddenly engulfed in an oven. Hearing screams and glimpsing the flicker of flames, I slithered out from under Terrac and scrambled to my feet.

The crops were ablaze, forming a wall of fire on either side. Through the dancing flames stretching toward the sky, I saw people dashing for cover. Terrac and I were separated from them by the flames.

I looked up to see the dragon turning in the air to make another pass, fire glowing in her throat as she opened her jaws in a roar that shook the earth beneath my feet.

My heart froze in my chest. Neither Terrac nor I were armed. I had not anticipated danger when I left Myria's cottage. So we were helpless to do anything but stand rooted to the spot, watching as the dragon spewed out another blast of flames that consumed the remaining crops.

All was chaos. Women and children ran, screaming, to the cliff's edge and clambered down the ropes toward the comparative safety of the village. My confused mind told me I should do something to help them, but I didn't know what. Everything was happening too quickly.

The dragon beat her broad wings, lifting higher into the sky. It looked as if she was retreating. But then she tucked her wings into her body and dove sharply down past the burning fields toward Swiftsfell.

"We need to get out of here!" Terrac shouted in my ear, his voice rising above the roar and crackle of the inferno. His sweat-streaked face was blurry before me as thick smoke clouded my vision and made my throat burn.

He took my arm and tried to push me toward the end of the row of burning stalks. But I came to a sudden halt, remembering.

Myria!

I whirled, looking for my grandmother. She had been only a short distance behind me mere moments ago. But now she was gone.

I shouted her name and pulled loose from Terrac's grip, rushing back to where I had last seen her. Acrid smoke filled my eyes, disorienting me. My skin was dry with the heat of the blaze. Burning stalks fell into my path, blocking my way.

Coughing, tears streaming from my eyes, I nearly stumbled over a charred corpse on the ground. The body, huddled face-down, was burnt almost beyond recognition. But I knew the yellow silk scarf in her hair, recognized the beaded belt around her waist.

The world seemed to stand still as, with a howl of pain, I dropped to her side. I was vaguely aware of the flames licking closer, of Terrac trying to drag me to my feet. But I could not take my eyes away from the charred body, could not reconcile what was before me with the living, breathing woman I had been talking with only minutes ago.

A rushing sound in my ears, I gasped for breath as the world around me erupted into showers of sparks and tongues of flame.

Terrac's strong arms were around me, lifting me away from the heat and the smoke. I closed my streaming eyes and gave in to the oblivion pulling me into shadow.

* * *

When I woke a few hours later, I was lying on a pile of blankets on the hard floor of Calder's study. There was no sign of Terrac, but Hadrian was at my side.

Other bodies filled every available floor space, and through the open door I could see more of them in the next room, weary, soot-stained people sleeping or holding their loved ones close.

Hadrian told me that after the dragon had burned the high field it had attacked the village. Many had lost their homes today and were crowded into Calder's undamaged house for shelter.

"Where's Terrac? Is he safe?" I asked quickly, my voice raspy from smoke exposure.

"He managed to get you both to safety," Hadrian reassured me. "He's out there now, helping to put out the fires. Everyone escaped from the high field, although many found no homes to return to."

"Not everyone escaped," I said dully, fighting an ache in my chest. "Myria is dead. I saw her."

Hadrian rested a hand on my shoulder. "Terrac told me. I'm sorry. I know you were only just getting to know her. Is there anything I can do?"

I swallowed. There was nothing anybody could do.

"Why did it happen?" I wondered aloud. "It was a peaceful day until the dragon came out of nowhere."

"The dragon, Micanthria, is an ally of the Drejian people in the mountains. It seems they wearied of waiting for Swiftsfell's late tribute and decided to send a message by destroying the village's crops and homes."

Throat tightening, hands trembling, I stopped hearing Hadrian's words. I kept seeing Myria's face as it had been in life. And then her blackened corpse. I had only just found my grandmother, and we'd had so much left to learn about each other. But now we never would.

Rage rushed through my veins and, with it, determination.

Chapter Six

The cliff path was treacherous by moonlight. In most places it was no more than a rough, downward sloping shelf etched into the rock face, scarcely wide enough for putting one foot in front of the other.

At a particularly steep point, I slipped, loose pebbles skittering from beneath my feet and tumbling over the edge into the nothingness. I would have followed them if my desperately searching hands hadn't found a tree root to catch hold of and steady myself. There were many of these scrubby little trees sprouting, seemingly impossibly, from crevices in the rock. Their presence was lucky because the original creators of this path had not considered it necessary to provide any manmade handholds to give travelers convenient purchase on the way down.

Continuing with renewed caution, I questioned my sanity for attempting this reckless descent. But it was too late to turn back now. Even if I could battle my way back up the steep incline, my absence from the village may already have been noticed, and my friends might well be turning every house upside down, searching for me. I could only hope they didn't guess my intent until it was too late.

I smothered a creeping sense of guilt, thinking of the stolen supplies I carried. While retrieving my weapons and original clothing from Myria's cottage, I had taken food from her cupboard. I knew she would not begrudge me that, but I couldn't say the same for the map I had taken from Calder's study. I wouldn't usually question such actions, but maybe I owed better to people who had befriended me. Maybe it was wrong to sneak away like a thief in the night.

But this was the only way. I could not share my plans, even with Terrac and Hadrian. If they knew where I went and why, they would try to stop me—or worse, join me. And it would be selfish to allow that. There was every chance I was headed to my death, and if that was the case, I couldn't drag the people I cared about down with me. This quest must be mine alone.

So as rapidly as I dared, I made my way down, straining to see into the shadows each time the moon dipped behind the clouds. I tried to visualize the way as it had appeared in daylight, but it had looked much different from the heights above with the rope railings on the Swiftsfell walkways safely between me and it.

As the sound of the rushing river below grew louder in my ears, I knew I was getting closer, even if it was too dark to make out the bottom of the gorge. I tried to remember where the boats were. I had noticed them this afternoon, a line of small green dots bobbing on the water where they were drawn up to the rocks.

I hadn't far to search. My feet had no sooner reached the end of the path where the ground leveled than I saw the shadowy shapes among the boulders.

I slung my traveler's pack into the nearest boat and, fumbling in the darkness, untied the vessel from its mooring. I was unprepared for the way the swift current instantly took hold of the craft and wrenched it away from shore. Quickly I splashed in after it, heedless of the swirling water rising to my waist. With one hand I caught the bobbing craft just before the water stole it away, and with an effort, I dragged myself aboard.

The boat dipped wildly from side to side, nearly capsizing, until I redistributed my weight. It was small, made to hold no more than one person, as evidenced by the single paddle I found at my feet. I picked the thing up and dipped it experimentally into the water. I had no experience steering boats, and this seemed the worst place to learn. Fully in the grip of the current, the vessel shot forward at alarming speed. I tried not to think what would happen if I fell overboard. I was a fair swimmer, but the quiet pools and meandering creeks of Dimmingwood were no comparison to what I faced here. I would be entirely at the mercy of the river.

Even now I could hardly see what lay ahead in the darkness and could only vaguely make out the cliffs rushing past on either side. If a floating log or other obstacle appeared in my path, I would be helpless to steer around it in time. Imagining the boat dashed against some rock and me dragged away by the stream, I asked myself again if I was making a huge mistake.

I half turned to look back at Swiftsfell, but the cliff village had already disappeared from view. It was just me and the swirling waters now as I plunged on into the night. I wondered if I would survive to see morning.

* * *

Dawn's first light found me cold, wet, and exhausted after a night spent battling the river. But at least I was alive. At the first shades of gray in the sky, I began scanning the shoreline anxiously. I had studied Calder's map until it was imprinted on my mind, and I knew exactly what landmarks to look out for.

It wasn't long before I recognized the first marker. The leaning tower of rock on the near shore jutted into the sky, rising higher than the cliffs to either side. I steered toward the shore, grateful the current had slowed some miles back, allowing me to maneuver the boat with relative ease.

The rocky landing rose in a steep incline. There was no gradual bottoming out. My craft simply slammed into the rock, and I had to leap immediately ashore. Half dragging, half lifting the boat after me, I was thankful for its lightweight construction.

When I straightened and looked around, the first thing I took in was the changed terrain. This landscape was even harsher than what I had left behind. Here there was no grass to be seen, and the only trees were low and scraggly and looked half-dead. Great cliffs rose on all sides, except directly ahead, where I could make out the purple shapes of mountains rising in the distance. The Arxus Mountains, marking the last border of the provinces, were my destination. When I stood on those mountains, I would be on unfamiliar ground, but my enemies would be all too comfortable there.

I swallowed. But this was no time to feel overwhelmed by the enormity of my mission or the low odds of success. I must keep going, one step at a time. So I refilled my waterskin, partially depleted from the long night. The land ahead was a desert place, and according to the map, there were few sources of water once I left the riverside. I summoned my resolve, shouldered my travelers pack, and set out.

* * *

It was midafternoon when I made my first stop. I had walked hours without rest, and the sun was now high in the sky. I took shelter in the shade of a tall boulder, where I had a few sips of water before chewing one of the rough strips of jerky I had brought with me.

Waves of heat rose from the rocky ground, reflecting the sun's rays and increasing my discomfort. I would have to be careful of my water supply. I wiped beads of sweat from my brow and closed my eyes for a second, envisioning the cool shadows of Dimmingwood.

Then I shook myself. The longer I sat here, the weaker I would grow and the more I would deplete my rations. I had to keep moving. My feet, unused to ground that alternated between sand and shale, ached in protest as I shouldered my waterskin and walked on.

I was so distracted by my discomforts that I did not immediately notice I was being followed. It came as a gradual realization, the feeling of unseen eyes watching me, the eerie sensation creeping down the back of my neck. I had felt this before leading up to the mysterious attack at the stream outside Swiftsfell. The half-healed wound between my neck and shoulder smarted at the memory. The dragon attack had driven from my mind the fact I was being tracked by a deadly stranger, but my fears were revived now.

Uneasily, I looked around. Nothing moved on the horizon. With no foe in sight, there was nothing I could do but continue on. Still, I cast constant looks behind me and felt a growing conviction it would not be long before my enemy made his next move.

* * *

A sudden noise bounced across the walls of a canyon, a sliding, shattering sound as if someone had unsettled a lot of rocks and sent them tumbling from a height. It was alarmingly close. I scanned the cliffs rearing up on either side of me. Anyone could be peering down on me from the safe vantage point of one of those ridges. But I glimpsed no flurry of movement and nothing out of place. The nervous feeling that I wasn't alone was growing stronger.

Intentionally dropping my waterskin and turning back to fetch it, I used the opportunity to look surreptitiously behind me. But here too there was nothing to be seen. Only the miles of rocky ground I had already traversed, with the constant rock walls and boulders lining the way.

I thought of the black-cloaked attacker who had nearly killed me only days before. I had not seen him coming until it was nearly too late. If he were following me again, he had an even better opportunity now to destroy me. I was utterly alone, having slipped away from the relative protection of my friends. And these surroundings were an ideal place for a bowman to hunt his prey. There was no place for me to run and few spots that would make suitable cover. Even now, he could be looking down from an outcropping or peering around a boulder, waiting for his perfect shot.

Hopelessly exposed in the open, it was all I could do not to make a mad dash for the closest shelter. But if my enemy had me in range at this very moment, the last thing I wanted was to alarm him into immediate action. Instead I forced myself to move slowly and casually to the towering rock wall along my path. I had spotted a big, shady cleft cut out of the wall, and as I climbed a pile of rubble to reach it, I unshouldered my traveling pack as if I planned to rest when I reached the top.

In the shadow of the cleft, I was sheltered from attack from most directions. No enemy could reach me here unless he dropped all subtlety and came at me directly. I had bought myself a few minutes to think, to form a plan. What I needed was to turn the tables on him, to know his exact position while leaving him guessing at mine. But how to accomplish that?

An unexpected tingling sensation brushed the edges of my consciousness. This wasn't the natural instinct that had first alerted me to danger. It was something different, that little tickle along my senses that said my magic had picked up the presence of another person. Startled, I reached into the loose neck of my tunic and drew out the glossy dragon scale from Myria. The augmenter dangled at the end of its chain. I was still learning to use the thing, still unused to drawing magic through this new source to bring my powers back to life. Did I dare trust it now?

I had no choice. It was telling me something, warning that my enemy was approaching from the same direction I had come. At least I now knew he wasn't ahead of me or stationed in the heights above.

I saw my opportunity. There was a tall pile of rocks against the crevice where I lurked. I scrambled to the back of the heap and began carefully scaling the rocks. Despite my caution, I sent streams of pebbles raining in all directions. I could only hope my pursuer did not see or hear the disturbances. From the top of the heap, I could look down on the cleft in the rock, where I'd hid only minutes ago. There was nothing to see yet, but I felt the approach of that other presence. His slowness signaled caution, hinting he was unsure what he would find ahead. Good.

I waited, pressed flat against the hot rocks, tension making the sweat stream from my pores. My mouth was as rough and dry as the desert sand, my heartbeat pulsing in my ears. Then I saw him. The black-cloaked figure approached my former hiding place, creeping toward the rocky crevice with the wariness of a hunter stalking his prey. If he knew I was no longer resting within the shadows, he gave no sign of it. I could make out little of him from this higher vantage point, could discern only that he was tall and young. His hood was thrown back against the heat, affording me a view of the top of his head and his close-cropped, brown hair.

But what commanded my attention above all else wasn't the young man but the weapon he carried. A longbow. I stared, transfixed. It couldn't be. Surely my eyes were failing me or the heat had driven me mad. There could be no other explanation for what I saw. For it was no ordinary bow he carried.

It was mine.

My old bow, enchanted with the twisted magic that had eventually forced me to discard it. Weeks ago, before setting out on this journey, I had tossed the thing into the falls above Red Rock, never to be seen again. Yet here it was now. I could feel it, could sense the life humming within it as I used to in the old days. It fairly glowed with a power of its own, a magic I remembered all too well. My mind rushed back to the broken arrow I had kept after the attempt on my life. No wonder it had emitted an almost tangible aura that I had been aware of despite the stunted state of my magic. It had come into contact with the bow, which I would recognize anywhere.

I shook myself and forced my attention back to the danger at hand. A fresh arrow was nocked to that bow now, and it was meant for me. I licked my lips and silently drew a knife from my sleeve. But my movement upset a nearby stone and sent it tumbling with a noisy clatter.

My enemy's head whipped around at the sound and he half turned, bow at the ready.

Chapter Seven

Unwilling to give him time to take aim, I leaped down on top of him. My weight slammed into him and bore us both to the ground. The impact of our collision knocked the breath from my lungs, but to remain motionless until I could breathe again would mean death. Ignoring the pain in my chest, I plunged my knife at my adversary's shoulder. But he recovered from his surprise in time to catch my wrist in midair and turn the blade away from him. Unable to twist free of his powerful grip, I fumbled with my free hand to draw my second knife. I stabbed it into the only place I could easily reach from this position, his upper thigh.

It was a glancing blow. I hadn't much strength to put into it, but it was enough. He screamed in pain, instantly releasing his grip on my wrist. In the same moment, I discovered I could breathe again and sucked in great gulps of air even as I wriggled off the prone form of my enemy and groped after the bow that had been knocked from his hands.

Writhing and clutching his injury, my enemy didn't try to stop me.

My fingers closed around the elderwood arm of the bow. Immediately my fears abated, and confidence surged through me. My feelings or those belonging to the bow? It didn't matter. When my other hand, fumbling in the sand, found the loose arrow it sought, I scrambled to my feet.

My opponent, finally realizing his predicament, unbent from his pained posture to grab at my legs, but I kicked free. Panting from the struggle, I stood over my fallen enemy and trained the arrow at him. It was strange, feeling the smooth elderwood in my hands again. But I couldn't let myself be distracted by the familiar sensations it awakened in me or by the soft, welcoming whisper I could almost hear stirring through the back of my mind.

"Tell me why you've been trailing me," I demanded of the stranger at my feet. "Why are you trying to kill me?"

He glared up at me with eyes that seemed, once again, hauntingly familiar.

Although he still gripped his wounded thigh, his anger was so intense he seemed to forget his pain and the blood trickling past his fingers. "I hunt you because I was paid to do it," he spat. "But I'd have taken the job for nothing, if only to avenge my father, dead at your hands. Or near enough by your doing as to make no difference."

I stared as questions tumbled around in my head. I had made my share of enemies in the past, but who could want me dead badly enough to hire an assassin to track me across the provinces? And more to the point, most of my enemies were the sort who would come after me themselves if they wanted to kill me. I couldn't think of anyone with the means or inclination to send this person.

Yet the words that found their way out of my mouth weren't about that at all. "Whose death do you speak of? Who was your father?"

My words sounded rough, but looking on a face as familiar to me as if I were seeing a ghost, my stomach squirmed.

His eyes were defiant. "My father was Brig. An outlaw of Dimmingwood."

The name, even though part of me had been expecting it, struck like a blow.

He sneered at my stricken expression. "I see you remember him now. Doubtless it's hard to forget a friend you betrayed to his death."

Even stunned as I was, I could not let that pass. "I never betrayed Brig," I murmured. "He was like a father to me, and I cared about him to the last. When he was dead, I killed the man who turned on him, a spy named Resid."

But I wasn't thinking about the explanation as I gave it. Instead my mind was yanked powerfully back into the past.

I was a small child, lying in a pile of moldy leaves in a cave hidden deep in the heart of Dimmingwood. Feigning sleep, I eavesdropped on the conversation of the two men standing over me.

"Brig, you know this child's not yours to keep, right?" one of them asked. "You understand she can't stay long in Dimmingwood? Your sons are gone and Netta with them. There's no bringing your family back or replacing them with this girl."

Right from the beginning, that was the first thing I learned of Brig, the man who saved my life and eventually adopted me. That he had once had a family, and they were gone. He would never speak of where they were or why they had left him, although others would gossip behind his back. Exactly what had become of his two small sons was always a mystery to me. Until today.

My mind was drawn back to the present by a disbelieving snort from the enemy before me.

"A convenient story," he said. "But I've heard better and from lips I trust more than yours."

"Whose would that be?" Past the initial shock, I was angry now. "Who invents such an evil charge against me? For I will stand any other insult but never the lie that I turned against Brig."

He did not give the name of my accuser, but a flicker of uncertainty crossed his face. Off his guard, his features no longer twisted in fury, his resemblance to Brig was striking. It was as if I had turned back time and stood looking at the man himself, twenty years younger than when I knew him. It was a sight to make my eyes sting and my throat tighten.

I wasn't aware of lowering my bow until I saw the youth reach surreptitiously for the dagger at his belt.

"Don't do it," I warned, training my arrow again at his heart. For a tense moment we stayed like that, he with his hand on the knife's hilt, me holding my breath, sweat trickling down my back as I prayed he wouldn't draw the weapon. Could I shoot him if I had to? Could I put an arrow through Brig's flesh and blood?

My expression must have said I was prepared to.

Slowly, reluctantly, he drew his hand away from the weapon. "So what happens now? Is this the part where you murder me, as you did my father?"

I didn't rise to the bait this time but ordered him to disarm very slowly and to toss me his waterskin. He obeyed, and after collecting his things, I backed away.

"Here's how this is going to play out," I told him, slinging his waterskin onto my shoulder to join my own. "My destination is a two-day journey across this wasteland. With an injured leg and no water, you'll never make it that far. Even if you were foolish enough to try, you're unarmed, and I would shoot you down the first time I caught you following me."

His eyes glittered with hate. "So you leave me to die in this desert?"

"There's nothing stopping you from binding up your leg and limping back to the river. It's a kinder option than you would have given in my place."

"If our positions were reversed, you would be dead by now and my father avenged."

He was either stupid or made fearless by his hatred of me. I didn't have the patience to deal with either possibility. "Your accusations are growing tiresome. I cannot make you believe that I had no hand in Brig's death, but I advise you to reconsider the trustworthiness of your source. Ask yourself what motive the one who hired you might have for lying about my past and seeking my destruction. What is he afraid of, that he is so eager to ensure I never return to Ellesus?"

"Ridiculous," he sneered. "A respected member of the Praetor's council has nothing to fear from the likes of you."

"Praetor's council, you say?" I mentally shuffled through my limited knowledge of the Praetor's advisers. My only glimpse of these exalted people had been on the occasion where I had made my ill-conceived attempt at assassinating their ruler. I had failed miserably and, in the end, had been forced to join the very man I had hoped to kill. There had been councilmen present for that, but none of them stood out in my memory. None had cause to act against me now.

My enemy looked annoyed at his slip. "Kill me if you want, but I'll tell you no more than that. I'll never disclose the name of the one who hired me."

"Then maybe you'll give you own?" His bravery reminding me of Brig, I softened slightly. Maybe he had more than appearance in common with his father.

He scowled, and I thought he would refuse me this piece of information too, if only to be obstinate.

But it seemed he had used up his store of defiance. "Martyn. I am Martyn."

"All right, Martyn. I have only one question more for you. How did you come to possess my bow?"

"Everyone knows of the famous bow belonging to Ilan of Dimmingwood," he said. "Your precious forest outlaws fished it out of a stream and were saving it in your memory. When I went sniffing around the outlaw band, looking for answers about my father's fate, I soon learned of the bow. People say it's the only weapon that can defeat you. So I took it, thinking it would be a fine irony to destroy you with your own bow."

"And so you nearly did." Privately, I was amused by the nonsensical idea that I was some unnatural being who could only be killed by a magical weapon. But I sobered, remembering this young man might be ignorant but he was still an enemy it would be unwise to turn my back on.

"For your father's sake, I am leaving you alive. That is more than I've ever done before with someone bent on killing me. I won't ask why you are suddenly so concerned with Brig's fate, when none of his kin seemed interested in him while he lived."

He tried to protest, but I cut him off. "You should tear off a bit of your cloak and wrap that wound tight before you lose any more blood. Then take yourself back home, wherever that may be. You have no honest quarrel with me, and I want none with you. But make no mistake. The next time I lay eyes on you, I won't hesitate to kill you."

I glanced at the sky where the sun was dipping behind a ridge. "And now I have a long way to go and not many hours left until dark. Good-bye, Martyn, son of Brig. I hope we do not meet again."

I left him there, sitting on the blood-spattered sand and looking after me in confusion. I offered up a silent apology to Brig and tried not to wonder what would become of his son.

* * *

Following Calder's map, it took me two more days of travel to reach the mountains. I never saw any sign of Martyn following me and wondered with a pang of guilt whether he had successfully retraced his steps to the river or if he was dead by now.

It was a rough climb up the mountainside. The air here was as dry as that of the desert I had left behind, but temperatures dropped the higher I went. I saw snow on the slopes above and hoped I would not have to go that far. I wasn't equipped for cold or for scaling steep peaks. Luckily, my map showed the Drejians' fortress at a lower level.

I had only been climbing for a day when I found myself on a craggy bluff overlooking a familiar prospect. It was exactly as the map showed, a place with high rock walls on three sides and a hill of shale on the fourth side leading up to a pile of boulders.

One of those tall rock walls was an entrance to the Drejian stronghold in the side of the mountain. The stone gates were high and wide. It was impossible to imagine them being opened by any outside force. Certainly it would take more strength than mine to budge them.

Equally intimidating were the two statues on either side of the gates, soaring rocks carved into the rough resemblance of winged men. I doubted Drejians were as tall as these were depicted, but even allowing for exaggeration, they were a fierce-looking enemy.

Fortunately it was not the Drejians I had come to face.

I had no sooner had the thought than my eye caught movement from below. Pacing before the entry to the Drejian fortress was a creature now familiar to me. Massive and black scaled, she was not just any dragon but *the* dragon. Micanthria. Just as I remembered her from the attack on the high field in Swiftsfell.

Memories of that day flashed through my mind. Again I heard the screams of the villagers, saw Myria's blackened corpse. Heat raced through my veins to rival the flames of the dragon. In my hatred, it was hard to think of anything but the need to destroy the creature before me. But some rational part of me knew I mustn't give in to the desire for vengeance yet. I had been no match for Micanthria then, and I would be none now. Not while she was on her guard.

So I bided my time and waited until daylight faded and the moon rose high in the sky. I watched while the dragon patrolled her ground, watched when she finally settled down to gnaw on the carcass of some large wild beast she must have killed earlier. When she had eaten her fill, I feared she would resume her watchfulness. But instead, she lay down against an outcropping of rock, lowered her head, and was still.

Now that it was safe to move without great danger of detection, I crept closer, scrambling as speedily as I dared down the side of the ridge. I was cautious, crossing near the mouth of the Drejian stronghold, but I needn't have been. There were no warriors in sight. Supremely confident in the strength of their dragon, these people apparently felt no need to post any other guard. It did not occur to them anyone would be foolish enough to come looking for a fight with Micanthria.

The immense bulk of the dragon loomed before me, a blue-black mountain of teeth and claws. I only had to get near enough so that I couldn't possibly miss my shot. It almost seemed too easy as I readied my bow and looked for the most vulnerable point to target. The head was best, I decided, drawing near. I would aim directly between the eyes.

I was so close I could almost have reached out and touched the creature, when a piece of gravel crunched loudly beneath my boot, breaking the silence of the night.

I froze, holding my breath, as one giant fiery eye snapped open to fix upon me.

In the back of my mind, a voice screamed at me to loose my arrow, but my numb fingers refused to obey the command. I stood paralyzed beneath the dragon's hypnotic stare. For a long, silent moment, the world seemed to stand still.

Then so quickly I barely saw it coming, Micanthria lashed out with one giant wing, catching me in the chest and throwing me a dozen yards to the side. I crashed into the ground with painful force and rolled, my bow knocked from my grasp and lost somewhere behind me.

I lay sprawled on my back, waiting for my head to stop spinning and for everything to come into focus again. Before I could regather my thoughts or my strength, hot dragon breath blasted over me, and I looked up into the gaping jaws of the beast. My hands moved to the knives tucked up my sleeves, even though I knew they would be little more than sharp splinters next to the gleaming row of huge teeth lowering toward me.

From nowhere, a thought slipped into my mind, as if Myria herself were tapping me on the shoulder and whispering what I must do. Instead of drawing my knives, I gripped the dragon-scale augmenter on its chain around my neck. Drawing on my rusty magical skills, I scoured my mind of all its fear and dread. I pushed these powerful emotions outward, away from me, and rolled them in a great wave to crash over my enemy.

Micanthria, poised to devour me, hesitated as the wall of magic hit her. Her eyes widened, growing glossy and dazed. If not fear, she was at least feeling confusion, and it was enough to distract her. Using the opportunity, I crawled from beneath her jaws and ran. A steep hill of shale sloped before me, and I scrambled desperately up the incline. My concentration broken, I felt the magic that held the dragon in confusion seeping away. Dissolving.

My fears were confirmed by the sound of pursuit from behind. The dragon was so much larger than I that it took her only a few strides to catch up to me. Her claws anchored her firmly into the side of the mountain while I struggled to keep my footing on the steep surface. Out of the corner of my eye, I saw her long neck stretch toward me, saw the approach of her great maw, filled with teeth glinting like ivory daggers.

I reached the summit and ducked between a pair of boulders, just in time to escape her reach. She was too big to squeeze in after me, but enraged, Micanthria butted her head against the rocks. I knew it was only a matter of seconds before her powerful blows would break apart my flimsy shelter.

But to my surprise, the attack did not continue. The dragon stopped smashing at the rocks and went strangely silent. After a moment, I gathered my courage and peered out to see what she was doing. To my horror, the dragon had reared and drew back her head. From around her jaws came a fiery glow, like flames about to burst out of the mouth of a giant oven. I watched her inflate her lungs, knowing I was about to be incinerated.

And then something happened. An indistinct shout sounded in the distance, a cry of challenge. In the next second, Micanthria arched her back and screamed in agony at some unseen attack. Eyes blazing, smoke billowing from her nostrils, the dragon rounded on her new foe.

It was then that I saw him at the foot of the rocks below. Martyn.

It couldn't be. In the moonlight, I could just make out his blood-soaked, bandaged leg. But he seemed not to feel the injury as he stood tall and brave with my bow in his hands.

When Micanthria wheeled on him, I saw the arrow protruding from her broad back. It could not have pierced deeply, having struck between her thick, gleaming scales. But it was obviously hurting her by the way she writhed her shoulders and flexed her wings in a futile attempt to dislodge it. Infuriated by the pain, she galloped down the mountainside.

Martyn never had a chance to dodge as she slammed her powerful wing into him. She caught him with the bone-spiked tip of her wing, and it punched through him like a spear. Then his limp body was tossed through the air to land in a motionless heap.

It all happened so fast I could only look on, stunned. My life had been saved by an enemy, and I had no time to wonder why. All that mattered was that Martyn had bought me time, and I must use it well.

I clenched my dragon-scale augmenter in my fist and tried to remember Myria's lesson, tried to remember how to draw on the skill my mother had excelled at. Sweat popping out on my forehead, I gritted my teeth and summoned lightning.

Chapter Eight

It was a small bolt of lightning I created, weak compared to the charge a more skilled magicker might have produced. But it shot through the air in a crackle of blue light and struck true against the base of a tall tower of rock nearby. The lower stones exploded in a shower of splinters and shards. The heavy rocks above suddenly had nothing to stand on and collapsed, rolling end over end down the mountainside.

Micanthria looked up, but in the path of the rockslide, she had only time to roar and spread her wings. Before she could take flight, the massive chunks of rock rained down on her with crushing force. In seconds, she was buried beneath the rubble.

I didn't wait for the last rock to come to rest before rushing down the slope. Only when I stood atop the mountain of debris with the dust settling did I realize the dragon buried beneath was not going to come bursting forth again. She was thoroughly dead.

I went to Martyn then. The brutal force of Micanthria's blow had knocked him safely free of the rockslide. But as I knelt where he sprawled on the ground, I knew he had escaped one death only for another. His chest was blood-soaked, and there was a ragged tear where the spike of Micanthria's wing had ripped through him. He could not live long.

He was conscious and, on realizing I was beside him, grabbed my arm, nails digging painfully into my skin.

"You spoke the truth? About my father?" he gasped painfully, as if there had been no break since our last conversation.

"I swear it."

"And he was avenged?"

"He was," I promised.

Martyn coughed, and spots of blood formed at the edges of his mouth. "I followed... because I had to know."

I imagined him determinedly crossing the desert on his injured leg, dragging himself from one water hole to the next these past two days, trying to keep up with me. All for an answer.

It was growing harder for him to speak, and he pulled me closer. "I have traded my life for yours... Repay me."

I winced at the urgency of his grip. "How can I do that?"

"My young brother, Jarrod. Look after him."

I nodded dumbly. I had no notion where I could find this Jarrod or what looking after him would entail. But I was in no position to refuse.

Martyn gazed past me, his expression growing fixed. I sensed his life slipping away, but I couldn't let him go yet.

"Wait! I need the name of the man who hired you in Selbius. The member of the Praetor's council who wants me dead."

But he was already gone, his hand on my arm growing slack and falling away.

Disturbed by the way his staring eyes still looked like Brig's, I drew down his eyelids. They would not stay closed, so I covered his face with his torn, blood-stained cloak.

Collecting my bow from the ground near his lifeless corpse, I felt hollow inside. This young man had not been my friend, had in fact spent most of our short acquaintance trying to kill me. But in the end, he had sacrificed his life for mine, even if it was only for the chance to question me. That combined with the memory of his father made it impossible for me to be indifferent to his death.

I became aware of the approach of several strangers and turned to face them. There were maybe a dozen winged Drejian warriors surrounding me, and as I watched, others poured out the mouth of their fortress.

The tightening of my grip on the bow was purely instinctive. There was little point in resisting against such numbers. I could only stand resigned as the Drejians ringed me, pointing spears and arrows my way.

* * *

It was my first-ever glimpse of these people, and they were an intimidating sight. Although I was not particularly short, they towered a good two feet taller than me. Their limbs and torsos were muscular, nearly twice the width of those of an ordinary person. Their leathery wings, even while folded as they now were, rose high above their bared shoulders and were tipped with sharp spikes of gleaming bone, much like Micanthria's. That was not the only resemblance they bore to the dragon. The faces were lean, cheekbones sharply prominent, and their necks and limbs were long. Their skin was leathery, with faint scaling patterning their faces and the backs of their arms. They had fiercely glowing, golden eyes and claw-like hands and feet.

For all that, intelligence shone from their eyes. They were more like men than beasts. And despite their unnerving appearance, their attitude was strangely cautious, as if they were reluctant to confront me. If they guessed I came from Swiftsfell, maybe they feared my magic. They could not know my power was now too drained to defend myself.

I waited to be killed.

Instead they disarmed me and bound my hands. Even the warrior who did this touched me as little as possible, looking as if he would rather keep his distance. I was then led by them through the gaping entrance of their stronghold, the great stone doors now standing wide open like the jaws of some hungry beast prepared to devour me. After I passed between them, I heard the doors groaning closed again. My shoulders tensed with the realization I was cut off from the outside world and all chance of escape.

All around, cold rock walls glistened with dampness while rough columns of granite soared to the shadowed ceiling. I was led through vast empty caverns that stretched so far into the mountain I couldn't make out where they ended. This was such a foreign place that I couldn't guess what I would encounter next. I was surprised to be escorted through a corridor and onto an unstable platform of timber banded with metal, suspended by chains disappearing into the darkness above and below. This space was only wide enough to hold a handful of us. The rest of my captors stayed behind, as the platform gave a sudden jolt with the grinding of pulleys and began to sink into the unknown abyss.

Deeper and deeper we descended into the bowels of the earth. With every level we passed, my spirits plummeted further. I could feel any hope of ever returning to the safety of the upper world slipping away. Even if I managed to break free of my bonds and my strong guards, I would only become lost in these warrens and caverns. Unlike my captors, I had no wings to fly to the surface, and I didn't know if I was strong enough to operate the pulley system they used for my benefit.

As the platform propelled us bumpily downward, its rusty chains screeching in protest, I vaguely made out a pale glow from the level we approached. We were slowing for this one. And it was different from the rest. The others had been lit by flickering torches placed intermittently along the walls. But those gave way here to the harsher light of glow-stones embedded in the rock. Their cold light illumined a cave vaster than any yet.

Unlike the previous caverns, the touch of human hands was evident here. These columns weren't natural towers of granite but were carved and etched with runes and likenesses of men and beasts. They were primitively done but probably considered ornate by Drejian standards. From what I had read in Calder's book of their culture, they typically rejected art and beauty as unworthy pursuits.

Our conveyance jerked to a halt, and I was hustled forward into what I guessed to be something like an audience chamber. Ahead there was a dais atop rows of stone steps, and occupying the dais were several empty seats. One was so big and high-backed I could only assume it was intended for a person of importance. I was permitted to advance only halfway across the room before my escort stopped me. One of them spoke in Drejian, a guttural tongue that was incomprehensible to me. I understood by his gestures that I was to stay where I was. Under my boots, a series of carved triangles intersected on the floor to form the pattern of a many-pointed star enclosed within a broad circle. Torches stood on high poles around this circle. They were rendered unnecessary by the cool light of the glow-stones, but maybe their purpose was ceremonial.

At the heart of the many-pointed star was a heavy metal ring attached to a chain. One of my guards looped the chain through the ropes binding my hands. Once I was secured, all the warriors faded back, leaving me alone in the empty, echoing chamber.

Only I wasn't really alone, because I quickly realized there were other, silent presences stationed in shadowy corners of the room. Servants perhaps. They were dressed simply, in sleeveless tunics that reached past their knees. They were unlike the warriors in that their heads were unshaven. And they had no wings, despite possessing other Drejian features. I wondered if their wings had been removed to symbolize their servant status or to show they belonged to a lesser class. Whatever the case, these dull, motionless observers showed no interest in me.

Since they all seemed to be awaiting something or someone, I stilled the nervous fluttering in my stomach and adopted a waiting stance myself. A sudden rumbling sound drew my attention across the room to where a pair of heavy doors slowly swung back. Through this entrance marched a small procession led by a tall figure clothed in red.

The first female Drejian I had seen, she was as tall and powerfully built as any of her warriors. Atop her shaven head rested a circlet with long strands of golden beads descending like a mane over her shoulders and flowing down her back. There was a scepter in her hand, and bracelets adorned her arms.

Flanked by a dozen others of her kind who I guessed were nobles or councilors, the queen mounted the dais and seated herself on the high-backed throne. When she surveyed me with her golden gaze, I tried to appear respectful but not overawed. Confident but not arrogant. It was a difficult manner to convey, and I had no idea whether I managed it.

One of the Drejian warriors who had taken me into custody stepped forward now, placing himself between me and the queen. After offering her a deferential gesture, he delivered a short speech in their strange tongue, probably a report on the cause and means of my capture.

Listening, the queen's eyes widened in surprise and, at one point, apparent anger. But she quickly recovered, a mask of cool boredom slipping over her face. When the warrior fell silent, she flicked her bony fingers, motioning him to one side. I saw that her claw-like nails were sharp and long.

Although I sensed through my dragon-scale augmenter that she was unnerved, the queen's expression was tranquil as she addressed me in my own language. "I am told you have trespassed on my lands, puny stranger, and that you have killed my dragon, Micanthria."

"That is true ..." I hesitated, trying to decide what honorific she was accustomed to before giving up.

"And you make no defense of these crimes?" she questioned. "Are you not aware that the sentence for a captured spy is slow death?"

"But I'm no spy."

Her eyes flashed. "Liar. I know what you are and whence you come. None but a filthy magicker could have defeated Micanthria. You are one of those cliff-dwelling rats from Swiftsfell."

I bit my tongue, remembering more lives than mine were at stake, and spread my hands in a pacifying gesture. "It is correct that I am a magicker with connections to the cliff-dwellers. It is on their behalf that I come."

"As an assassin," she accused. "Here to destroy my beautiful and terrible Micanthria."

My mind raced. A dangerous plan was beginning to form in my head, and there was no time to consider whether it was good or bad.

"Come to *execute* Micanthria," I corrected, "for the killing of my grandmother. But I have another purpose as well. I am here as a representative of Swiftsfell, to arrange an agreement that will see the end of the Drejian attacks on that village."

At this, the queen's surrounding companions began whispering among themselves.

She ignored them as, eyes narrowed, she asked, "You have authority to speak for the cliff-dwellers?"

"Absolutely," I lied.

"It will take a very high price to diminish my wrath after the destruction of my dragon. Swiftsfell's tribute is doubled."

I took a chance. "I haven't traveled all this way to pay the gold demanded. I had come instead to claim the ancient right of judicial combat."

Throughout the room, all whispers fell silent and a hush descended.

The queen's face was hard and her voice strained, yet I sensed a twinge of secret alarm. "What know you, puny magicker, of judicial combat?"

In my mind's eye, I saw again the pages of Calder's book. I hoped I remembered their contents correctly. "Drejians follow a strict honor code in the resolution of legal disputes. A part of that code allows for a wronged party to challenge their adversary in an ordeal of strength. A trial by combat, with the Drejian gods ensuring victory for the just party."

I took a breath and hoped I wasn't going to regret what I was saying. "I charge you, Queen of the Drejians, with ordering the dragon Micanthria's attack on Swiftsfell, thus bringing about the wrongful death of my kinswoman. I demand justice by judicial duel."

The queen laughed sharply, casting a quick glance toward her noble companions. "You reveal your ignorance of our ways, magicker. The challenge to a trial by battle can only be issued to and by persons of Drejian birth. Your inferior, wingless race possesses no rights under our law."

I winced at the blow to my plans.

But a flurry of whispers had resumed from those surrounding the queen. One of her companions spoke up, and I wondered if it was significant that he spoke in my language, so that I could understand his words to the queen.

"With respect to your Magnificence," he said, "tradition dictates that if a wingless stranger has proven himself a courageous opponent, he may be granted the right of combat. Many would say that, in slaying Micanthria, this magicker has demonstrated worthiness."

The queen scowled at the speaker. "You know this is a questionable challenge, Prince Radistha. I mark you as its supporter."

It seemed I was benefitting from some personal or political undercurrent I did not understand. But I didn't need to know the root of the discord between this Radistha and the queen to use it to my advantage. Quickly I said, "I am certain her Magnificence does not seek to hide behind technicalities to avoid this ordeal. Surely the justice of her cause gives her faith in the trial's outcome?"

Judging from the scorching look the queen shot me, I was pushing too far. But a glance at her nobles revealed thoughtful expressions and nodding heads. Some, at least, were looking favorably on my words.

But just as I was beginning to hope, one of the nobles broke in with a sharp protest. Because it was in the Drejian tongue, I was left to guess at what he said. But his outraged tone and scathing glares in my direction made it obvious he was protesting my challenge. A heated dispute broke out among all the noble companions.

I sensed events were veering off course and that my chance was slipping away from me.

The queen, never looking away from her advisors, made an impatient motion with her hand. One of the Drejian warriors took that as his signal to unfasten me from the floor ring that had held me to the spot.

I was unable to accept that my audience could end so abruptly. "Wait! What's happening?" I demanded as the guard prodded me away. "I will not leave before my challenge is answered!"

The winged warrior either could not or would not answer. As for the queen and her nobles, they were locked in debate, and spared my protesting departure no notice. With the sinking knowledge that my final ploy had failed, I had no choice but to be led through a side entrance out of the chamber. I wondered what was planned for me next. Imprisonment? A hasty execution?

Chapter Nine

Wordlessly, my captors brought me down a series of twisting tunnels and then an endless flight of steep stairs. It looked like we were entering a less inhabited area now. The air was cold and damp, and a draft came from somewhere. Our path grew rougher and narrower, so that my tallest guards had to stoop and draw in their wings to avoid the walls and ceilings. If they had forgone flying in favor of walking for my benefit, they now did so for their own. There could be no swooping or gliding through these tight spaces. Glow stones became more infrequent, until finally we passed no more at all and would have been left in utter darkness if some of my escort had not taken up torches. Wherever we were going, it was apparently a place where illumination was an unnecessary luxury.

My uneasiness grew.

At length, a solid boulder appeared in our path, and we stopped before it. I didn't realize until several warriors combined their strength to roll the rock aside that it acted as a strong door, blocking a small entrance into the chamber beyond. It was a tight doorway that would barely have admitted a large man. My guards showed no intention of entering it. Instead they cut the ties binding my hands and indicated I should pass through alone.

I wondered what would happen if I refused. They had seemed reluctant to handle me roughly thus far, possibly fearing whatever magic had been powerful enough to defeat their dragon. But my power was still weak from its last use, and I was not eager to test the warriors.

I did as they wanted, ducking through the narrow space and into the next chamber. Here it was pitch black so that I couldn't see what kind of room I had entered. I wondered if I was expected to wait indefinitely in the dark. But after a moment, one of the Drejians thrust his arm, bearing a flaming torch, into the space. Its flickering light illuminated a circular cave, most of it taken up by an immense, gaping pit at its center. If one kept close to the walls, there would be just room enough to walk a circle around that pit but not much more than that. There were no obvious entrances or exits to the room beyond the one I had just taken.

The Drejian guard did not follow me into the cavern but grunted and indicated I should take the torch from his hand if I did not want to be left in the dark. He was the same warrior who had fastened me to the ring in the audience hall and who had "introduced" me before the queen.

Taking the offered torch, I asked, "Is this to be my prison then? For how long?"

His shrug might have meant that he didn't know or simply that he didn't care. Neither possibility was reassuring.

When he had gone, I watched as the other guards rolled the heavy boulder back into place, effectively sealing me into the tomblike chamber.

I shivered at the draft coming from the yawning pit and cautiously approached the edge as closely as I dared. I peered down into the black abyss. There was no telling what was down there. The only clues were the softly whistling gusts of cold air wafting up and the constant sound of dripping water in the distance. Tearing a strip off my sleeve, I lit it against my torch and dropped the burning fabric down into the deep hole. I watched the blazing rag spiral downward until it shrank in the distance and I could see it no more.

That question was answered then. I was half-relieved to know I would not be escaping this dungeon by climbing down the mouth of the pit. I walked the perimeter of the room, following the circular walls and cautiously avoiding the places where the floor inclined inward, as if inviting me to slip and fall into the hole at its center. Despite my initial impression of a wide space, there was little floor room in the cavern, the pit taking most of it. I did not take long to finish my circuit and return to where I had started.

Enough time had passed that I guessed the Drejians had dispersed. Unless, of course, they had left a warrior or two behind to guard me. But I decided to take a chance. I set my torch against the wall to free both hands and then leaned with all my strength into the boulder. Sweat quickly broke out on my skin as I pushed at the rock until my arms were weak and trembling. But the boulder would not budge. Not even a little. Gasping to recover my breath, I realized it would take many strong hands to dislodge the obstacle.

Frustrated, I sank to the cold floor and gazed up at the grate in the rocky ceiling far overhead. I could almost imagine a faint, whitish illumination filtered through the grate from the glow stones on the next level. I hoped I was right because my single torch would not last forever. I tried not to guess how long it would be before the flames guttered out and plunged me into solitary darkness. For how many hours, days, or years, I wondered, would I be left to linger in that state? Would I ever see daylight again? Would I ever walk along the dappled paths of Dimmingwood again?

Fighting despair, I lay back and tried to rest. The past few hours had been physically and emotionally draining. I needed to recover my strength and wits in order to be ready at the first opportunity of escape.

I did not close my eyes though, watching through heavy lids as the torch burned itself down. I would not close my eyes until the last light had gone and darkness closed in.

* * *

I dreamed of Terrac. In my mind, I clearly saw the hot desert sun beating down on him, its dazzling rays reflected from a nearby pool of water. I recognized the puddle-sized watering hole as one I had passed during my trek across the desert. My heart swelled with hope at the realization Terrac was following my trail.

But something was wrong. He was lying out flat in the sand, eyes closed, body stiff. For a horrifying instant, I thought he was dead. Then I saw that his chest moved. He breathed quickly, shallowly, as if in pain.

A shadow appeared upon his pale face, and then Hadrian leaned over him, spreading a wet cloth across his brow. The warrior priest's voice was grave as he said, "I've done my best to magically isolate the venom in your hand, but I have not the skill to draw it out. We must get you to a healer quickly."

Terrac's eyes squinted open, and he said faintly but determinedly, "I'm not returning to Swiftsfell without Ilan. She's out here somewhere, lost in the burning desert or confronting the dragon's people, and she needs my help. I should have known she would do this. I should have prevented her from setting out alone."

Hadrian scrubbed a hand over his sweaty sunburned face, leaving behind streaks of grit. "There's no use blaming ourselves. Anyway, you are in no state for rescuing anybody. You're suffering now and only going to get worse."

Terrac opened his mouth and clamped it shut again, jaw flexing in pain. "It burns," he admitted.

"A fierce burning sensation is one of the side effects of a desert viper's venom, and it will only get worse as it travels through your body. Another effect is hallucinations. Soon you'll be unable to think clearly or make rational decisions. That is why we must turn back now—"

He broke off abruptly, looking around with a sudden puzzled expression, as though sensing my unseen presence. Then he looked directly at me.

"Ilan?" he mouthed, clearly startled.

"Hadrian!" Straining my magic, I tried to reach out to him. I had to communicate, had to tell him to forget me and save Terrac.

But our connection was tenuous, and as I struggled to maintain the link, I could feel it disintegrating. I got one last look at Terrac's face, twisted in pain. Then he, Hadrian, and the entire scene disappeared from view.

I came back to my world with a cold rush of awareness. I was sprawled on the hard floor of the cavern, trapped in utter darkness and helpless to rush to the aid of my friends.

Or… did they really need my help? I tried to calm my desperate emotions and consider the possibility my dream had been nothing more than a vivid nightmare. It wasn't as if I had been prone to visions before. There had been occasional memories or fears wrapped within dreams, stirring to the surface at crucial times to nudge me in the right direction. But never anything like this. Why now?

Frustrated, I thumped my fists against the stone. I couldn't take the chance the vision wasn't real. I had to get out of this place, not in a few hours or days, but immediately. No matter what had occurred between us back in Swiftsfell, my feelings for Terrac remained strong. If his life depended on me, I could not fail him.

But although he was only a few miles away, we may as well have been on opposite sides of the world. I was buried under a mountain, hopelessly sealed in this black tomb until the Drejian queen or someone else remembered my existence.

I got up and with new determination tried to recall exactly how I had summoned the lightning to defeat the dragon. After a moment's intense effort, I shaped the magic into what I envisioned and let it go.

A streak of blue fire shot through the cavern and disappeared down the gaping mouth of the pit.

It had only lasted a second, and when it was gone darkness returned. I blinked, spots dancing before my eyes from the brief illumination. After a moment's pause, I concentrated and tried again. This time I directed the lightning bolt, not into the abyss, but toward the boulder blocking my door. It blazed through the darkness, and sparks showered as it struck its target. Bits of debris rained down around me. But it was not enough. The lightning had been weak. I directed more bolts and, in the intermittent flashes of crackling fire, saw that I was steadily chiseling away at the stone.

I was also making a thunderous noise that must surely alert every Drejian within hearing distance. Imagining them running down the dark passages toward me, I summoned the most powerful lightning yet and slammed it into the boulder. Instantly, the rock exploded with a deafening noise, shattering into a million pieces.

I hoped light would come flooding through the open entrance, but it did not. The tunnel beyond was as black as the inside of the cavern. And creating more lightning to reveal my path was impossible. I had depleted my store of magic for the moment, and even my dragon-scale augmenter could not restore my strength. My knees too felt strangely weak, a sensation I remembered from the last time I had drawn on too much power—the time back in Dimmingwood when I had burnt myself out.

Shakily I felt my way through the door, leaving my prison behind, and stumbled blindly down the outer passage, trying to remember which way I had come. From ahead there came the sudden thudding sounds of many feet rushing my way. A distant light appeared from that direction. The Drejian guards were coming.

Chapter Ten

I had not thought my escape through, had proceeded without any plan beyond breaking out of my dungeon. But it was too late to form a plan as my enemies approached. All I could do was make my way in the opposite direction as swiftly as possible in the darkness. I could only guess what lay at the end of this passage, but it didn't matter. There was only one way to run.

I hadn't gone far, groping along in the dark and stumbling into walls, before I rounded a corner and slammed into another party of guards coming from the other way. I tried summoning lightning to throw at them, but all I managed was a weak blue flame that crackled around my fingertips before fizzling out. The guards seized me and shoved me face first into a wall. They no longer seemed concerned with handling me too roughly and held my wrists firmly, as if my hands were weapons that might erupt with more charges of lightning at any moment.

They dragged me back to the dungeon I had escaped, and when we encountered the shattered boulder, they fired excited questions in their strange language. I gathered by their tones and gestures that they wanted to know how I had destroyed the thing, but I could only shrug, not knowing how to explain.

They debated among themselves, and I got the feeling they were unsure what to do with a prisoner who couldn't be held by their strongest cell. They soon came to a decision and led me away down the tunnel again. For a long time we walked, leaving the prison area and eventually venturing into a rough-hewn passage that appeared to have been seldom traveled. Because of the empty carts we passed, I thought of an abandoned mine, although I had seen nothing yet in this mountain that appeared worth mining. I couldn't guess why they were bringing me here.

We didn't progress far before pausing in a storage area, where barrels and broken tools were layered with dust and draped with cobwebs. In the floor here there was a rusty grate, and someone threw this back to reveal a hole that was little more than a crawlspace carved into the rock below. They indicated I was to lower myself into this and, when I tried to refuse, prodded me with a spear until I had no choice but to do as they wanted. My feet had no sooner touched the bottom than they started to close the grate, and I had to duck or be struck in the head. I crouched beneath the low ceiling and peered up through the bars as my guards locked me in and dispersed.

At least I was not left in the dark this time, for there were flecks of glow stone imbedded in the walls above, perhaps to illuminate the way of those long-ago miners. My position now was worse than before. The walls of my new cell were so narrow that I couldn't lie stretched out without both ends of me touching opposite walls. Fighting the creeping sensation the rock was closing in on me, crushing me, I took deep breaths to calm myself. I had never been good with tight, enclosed spaces. To sooth the panic stalking around the edges of my mind, I reassured myself that I would not be in here long. As soon as my magic restored itself, I would break out of this cell as I had the last.

But as the hours passed and my magic slowly returned, I found there was a sort of wall separating me from it. Over and over I attempted to summon the blue lightning, but I could not. This was unlike anything I had encountered before, and I was reminded briefly of an exercise Hadrian had once taught me involving the blocking of magic. I could still sense the power flickering on the other side of that invisible wall, but I was helpless to touch it.

Since acquiring Myria's dragon scale, I was growing used to having magic again, and it was frightening to lose it. But clearly the Drejians had found some mysterious way to cut me off from my power. I could see no other explanation.

It hadn't taken me long to become familiar with my tiny cell, but I explored it more closely now as I realized my next escape might have to be by nonmagical means. There was little to examine. The walls were thick and solid, the floor constructed of the same material. The only way in or out was by way of the grate overhead. But it was strong and barely moved when I pushed and pulled at it. I even tried bracing my back and shoulders against the sloping wall and kicking at the thing, but the only result was a clanging noise that resounded hollowly down the mine shaft.

By the time I gave up, my mouth was dry and I was sweaty from my efforts. My rumbling stomach told me it had been a very long time since my last meal. By now I guessed I had been underground for around a full day, although it was hard to be sure without the passing of sun or moon to mark the time.

I slept for a while and did not dream this time. I was awakened by a rattling of the bars above. The grate was thrown back, and an expressionless face appeared above. The Drejian guard did not speak but tossed some objects down at me before quickly slamming the grate closed.

"Wait!" I shouted after him. "How long am I going to be down here?"

But he ignored my plea, and I heard his footsteps moving away.

In the dim light, I examined the items he had left me. There was a skin filled with water and a brittle, grainy substance that smelled like corn but had been hammered into a flat sheet. I nibbled at it, finding it tasted well enough and, more importantly, filled my aching stomach. I'd also been given a bucket, presumably for relieving myself. Although I wrinkled my nose, I was in no condition to reject the small favor. I had been enclosed in this place for an awfully long time.

Soon I curled up on the stone floor and slept again. There was little else to do in this place. When next I woke, it was to the sound of voices. The grate was thrown back, and there were several Drejians looking down on me this time. They indicated I should come out of my cell and offered their hands to assist me. But it didn't escape my notice that several kept weapons trained on me as if expecting trouble.

Most of these Drejians were the same guards I had encountered before, but there was one who was different. This aging, silver-haired man was unarmed and lacked the bearing of a warrior. His face was dignified, but his simple clothing suggested his social status was only middling. These things I took in with a glance, but there was something more unusual that arrested my attention. Although this Drejian had the features of his race that were fast growing familiar to me, including the leathery skin and light scaling, he lacked one obvious aspect. Like the servants in the queen's audience chamber, he was wingless.

I realized he was examining me even as I studied him. After a moment, he spoke fluently in my tongue. "My name is Kinhira, first servant of the exalted Prince Radistha. I have come to take you under the custody of my master."

It was a relief to finally be facing someone I could understand and who could understand me. I poured out my questions. "What is to become of me now? No one has told me anything. For how long am I to be a prisoner, and what has been decided of my challenge to duel the queen?"

He inclined his head and said gravely, "I realize you are eager for answers, but I can offer you none at this time. My understanding is that your situation is under debate by Queen Viranathi and her noble council and that your ultimate fate remains undecided. Until this changes, my ever-merciful master has intervened on your behalf so that you need not suffer these miserable confines. The exalted Radistha has made generous arrangements for you to be released into my personal charge."

Radistha. I recognized the name but could not think how I came to know it.

"Who is this Radistha, and what is his interest in me?" I asked.

The servant darted a quick glance to the guards on either side of us. "It is not for me to speculate on my master's intentions. I can only suggest that you accept his generous offer to dwell in the home of his servant until your fate is decided. My home is humble, but I think you will find it more agreeable than these quarters."

There was no arguing with that. I allowed myself to be led away by this Kinhira with my Drejian guards bringing up the rear.

"We have only a brief stop to make on our way," Kinhira informed me as we traveled. He was mysteriously silent on what that stop would be, but I offered no questions because my thoughts were consumed by another, more urgent matter.

As we left behind the abandoned mine shaft, I was aware of an unexpected weakening of the wall that had been blocking me from my magic. I was still unable to summon my power, but with every step we took, I felt I was closer to doing so. Had it been something about my cell or about the mine itself that had created that separation, cutting me off from my magic? I could feel the barrier fading now as we put distance behind us. Not wanting to alert my guards, I showed no outward sign of noticing the change. But carefully, silently, I tested the bounds of my strength.

We boarded another of the vertically moving platforms I had ridden earlier. It elevated us to a higher level, and we disembarked into a vast cavern unlike any I had seen yet. The place buzzed with people. Their clothing was ragged and worn, their faces dirty. And they too lacked dragon-like wings, seemingly signaling their lowly status.

Kinhira seemed in a hurry to reach our destination, and he led the way so quickly I formed only hasty impressions of the people we passed. But I noted there didn't seem to be any children or old people among them. These were fit, muscular men and women, all of them busily employed in various types of heavy labor. The air was heavy with the reek of so many sweaty bodies, and the noise of their hammers and rock-hewers and other tools echoed from wall to ceiling.

I was taken past all this commotion to where a pair of men worked at a forge. With long tongs, they pulled chunks of hot metal from the fire and pounded them with hammers, fashioning them into various shapes. These smiths treated Kinhira respectfully, maybe out of deference for his master, and put aside their work to give us their immediate attention. Although I could not understand their conversation with Kinhira, it didn't take me long to realize the nature of our business.

One of the smiths motioned for me to place my foot atop a block, and when I complied, his partner quickly fastened a metal band around my ankle, hammering pins into the shackle to hold it tight and secure. This was no ordinary constraint. It was constructed of an unfamiliar material, black and glossy and lightweight. Although very thin, it was surprisingly sturdy and unbendable. The instant the metal was brought close enough to be clamped around my ankle, I felt a strange, muffled sensation. It took me a second to realize what it was. And then I knew.

I was cut off from my magic again. Once more, the wall was in place.

* * *

My confusion must have shown on my face because Kinhira explained. The shackle I wore was made of a material common in the mines called nathamite. A peculiarity of the largely worthless material was that nathamite had a strange effect on magickers, blocking their ability to access their powers while in its close proximity. My jailers must have remembered this little-known fact after my escape from my first cell and so moved me to the mines, where the nathamite deposits in the rock would block my abilities.

Kinhira seemed to have plenty of faith in the nathamite. No sooner was it secured around my ankle, than he dismissed the guards accompanying us. They seemed reluctant to go, eyeing me as if, even unarmed and magickless, I might be a threat. But in the end, they went. After their departure, Kinhira took me away from the smiths and from the noise and bustle of all the workers. We traveled to a neighboring cavern, where the din of the distant laborers became only a vague echo in the distance.

Here there were small homes huddled closely together, often sharing walls or even stacked atop one another. Constructed plainly of blocks of crushed rock and tar, they blended into the black stone around them and looked very gloomy. Kinhira's home was little different than the others except that it was larger and had multiple rooms, possibly a sign that his position in his master's service was less humble than the station of his neighbors.

There were few people around except for a handful of ragged children playing in front of the houses. These Drejian younglings stared at me with curious eyes as Kinhira led me up the steps into his house.

We were greeted by a slim female of perhaps thirty years of age, whom Kinhira introduced as his daughter Tadra. Tadra was apparently the only family member who shared this home, and she kept the house for her father. She spoke my tongue, although not as well as Kinhira did. All the while she showed me around the sparsely furnished home, including the kitchen where I would sleep, her expression was anxious. I suspected she would have preferred not to have this foreign, potentially dangerous stranger staying under her roof.

* * *

During the next few days that followed, I got to know both Kinhira and his daughter better and found them decent enough folk, for Drejians. Tadra must have sensed how it grated on me that, as a condition of this more lenient confinement, I was never permitted to set foot outside the home. Setting aside whatever doubts she might have, she did her best to occupy me with household tasks, taught me simple words of the Drejian language, and tried to make me feel at ease.

Relaxing was something I could not do, not while my future was uncertain and while I continued to be haunted by nightmares about a suffering Terrac. But I made no more ill-considered escape attempts. It wasn't only the magic-blocking nathamite band around my ankle that held me here. I now realized how foolish I had been to think I could run away. My slaying of the queen's dragon had given her more motive than ever to hate Swiftsfell. If I escaped now, I would provide her with yet another reason to punish the magicker village.

During the long nights when I slept on a cushion before the kitchen fire, I was haunted by indistinct visions of Terrac, feverish and slipping in and out of consciousness beneath the burning desert sun. I dreamed also of Myria, and in my dreams my grandmother was alive again. She admonished me to think not of my safety or my fears for Terrac but of the Swiftsfell inhabitants whose lives might depend on my actions here.

No, running away was no longer an option. I must bide my time and plot ways to get near the queen again. I did not have long to wait for my opportunity.

One afternoon, I was watching Tadra in the kitchen as she prepared the corn cakes that were a common part of the Drejian diet. She was just pulling the cakes from the fire when her father came home unexpectedly early. During my short time in their home, I had learned that Kinhira invariably departed early in the morning to attend his master at some place called the hall. Usually he did not return until dinner.

But today he was home early and seemed agitated. He would not say why but made us contain our curiosity until after the noon meal. Only then did he invite me to join him before the fire in a game of spar. Spar was a Drejian amusement, played on a multicolored wooden board with moveable carved figures shaped like dragons and chimeras. There did not seem to be much strategy to the game, but the rules were confusing and changeable.

Kinhira's mind was not on the match, and I realized it when he allowed me to beat him at the first round.

"Something consumes your thoughts," I said, watching him reset the board.

He frowned. "My master is hosting an event at the hall this evening. The queen and her nobles will attend, and there will be feasting and festivities in her honor."

"And this troubles you?"

"It troubles me because it is no ordinary feast." He glanced up from the board, his gaze unexpectedly sharp. "It is commonly known that there is little friendship and even smaller trust between Prince Radistha and his stepsister, the queen. Now he professes a wish to mend the relationship."

"But this reaching out to the queen is only a ploy," I guessed.

Kinhira rubbed his chin, reminding me briefly of Hadrian, who employed the same gesture when deep in thought. "Can I trust your discretion in this matter?" he asked.

"Who would I talk to?" I returned. "I see no one except you and Tadra and go nowhere."

"Very well. The fact is there was a time when many people felt my master had a greater claim to the throne than his stepsister, Queen Viranathi. He has long been a thorn in her side, but she dares not rid herself of him because he holds the favor of many. Likewise, he dares not rebel against her until he is certain he has the support to guarantee an easy victory. His position has long been a precarious one. But I believe he saw the light of hope on the day you killed the dragon Micanthria and walked into that audience chamber to challenge the queen."

"I have never understood why he took an interest in my fate and arranged my removal from prison into your custody," I said.

"My master has been working quietly to keep you alive and in the memory of the nobles, when the queen would prefer you dead or rotting in her dungeons."

"But why?"

Kinhira contemplated the spar board on the table between us. "You offer Prince Radistha an opportunity to subtly rid himself of his rival. And in a just manner none could protest, not even if they see his hand behind her downfall."

I began to understand. "So I am a means to an end?"

"An end that could benefit you as much as my master," Kinhira pointed out quickly. "For while he might gain the queen's rule, you would attain your goal. I have been instructed to promise you life, freedom, and safety for your Swiftsfell friends. Radistha will consider their tribute paid and hostilities between our peoples resolved. You have only to play your part in his scheme."

I leaned forward. "If I do this thing, it will be for my own reasons, not for your master's."

Kinhira shrugged. "Your motives matter nothing to Prince Radistha. Only your results."

"And how can Radistha help me achieve those?"

"By providing you access to the queen. This is why he hosts the feast tonight, why Queen Viranathi is a guest, and why you will be among the servants waiting at her table."

"What? Can it really be that simple?" I asked.

"You are a curiosity whose presence will amuse the guests. A wingless, pale-skinned foreigner, a slayer of dragons, and a brave challenger of queens. Prince Radistha needs no better excuse to have you there."

I considered what he was suggesting. I had wanted an opportunity to get close to the Drejian queen, and this Prince Radistha, questionable ally though he may be, had the power to supply it.

"Tell your master," I said, "that we have a deal."

Chapter Eleven

The hall where Prince Radistha's feast was held that night was of a similar size to the queen's throne room, but its furnishings were less austere. Or maybe it was only the noisy crowd of revelers and the merry atmosphere that made this occasion seem so different from that other. The chamber was filled with tables and seats placed so close together that the celebrants were crowded elbow to elbow, and the busy servers had to navigate the room with care. I was one of those silver-tunicked servers, wearing borrowed Drejian-style clothing from Tadra and bustling among the crowds, refilling plates and cleaning spills and keeping tankards full.

I felt conspicuously foreign and out of place with my shorter stature and pale skin and hair, so different from the company around me. I refused to assume the deferential manner of the Drejian servants, and my surly countenance attracted still more attention. Kinhira had been right when he said I would be a curiosity to these folk. As I dodged between tables, bearing trays of food and pitchers of *skeil*, I heard the murmurs behind me, felt the stares on my back. I had picked up only a few words of their tongue from Tadra, but I knew enough to make out that the people I waited on were interested in me and speculating on the reason for my presence. My attendance here, even in the role of servant, danced dangerously close to offering offense against the queen I had so recently angered.

The queen. Since the start of the festivities, I had kept an eye on the big table at the head of the room where she was seated with Prince Radistha and a lot of other important persons. I tried not to lose my courage, but all the while I wondered, would my chance ever come? And if it did, was Radistha's plan too bold?

I was about to find out. I had kept my distance up to now and had yet to draw Queen Viranathi's notice. But there was Radistha catching my eye from across the room and casually lifting his tankard for a refill. I recognized this as my excuse to approach. Carrying a silver pitcher of *skeil*, I mounted the steps to the head table. The queen was at Radistha's right hand, engaged in conversation with her companions, but she broke off speaking to them when her gaze fell on me.

"What is this?" she asked Radistha, her voice rising. "Why comes this wingless magicker into my sight?"

Radistha feigned surprise. "Apologies if I have erred, my queen. But I was short on servers and thought the presence of this strange-looking dragon slayer would amuse the guests."

Queen Viranathi's lips drew back in a scowl. "It is not enough she lives and walks free after insulting your queen and destroying the dragon Micanthria? Now you wish me to accept her presence at feasts?"

Radistha's smile was ingratiating, as though he feared he had dared too much too quickly. "I had not realized my queen's anger burned so hotly. But of course, if the sight of this foreign dog displeases Your Magnificence, she will be removed."

My heart beat faster. My ally might be frightened into changing course at the first sign of conflict, but I would not. One way or another, I would resolve matters tonight. Ignoring Radistha's flick of the wrist signaling me to withdraw, I slammed my pitcher down on the table and placed myself squarely in front of the queen.

Making my voice loud enough for the whole table to hear, I addressed my enemy boldly. "I cannot help but wonder why my presence so disturbs Your Magnificence. Can it be because she does not care to remember that my challenge still awaits a royal answer?"

The queen's face twisted with distaste. She spoke not to me but to Radistha. "Are you behind the words of this puppet, Radistha? You persuade me to spare her life so that you may use her against me?"

Radistha's expression was wounded. "You do me a great injury, Your Magnificence. What interest have I in this matter but to see justice done? If this wingless creature has wronged you, I am as eager as any here to see her destroyed in a judicial duel, as the law dictates."

His tone was conciliatory, but I knew it was no accident he had left me an opening. I pounced on it.

"You see?" I said to the queen. "Your people have faith that you will meet the demands of custom and honor by accepting my challenge. But I? I have no such faith." For the benefit of the onlookers, I switched to the Drejian speech Tadra and I had practiced. "My opinion is that you fear to meet me in combat for you know I would destroy you as easily as I did your pathetic dragon."

A hush descended on the room, as every eye in the place fixed on our encounter.

Face contorting with rage, the queen leapt to her feet and stabbed a bony finger at me. "You do not deserve the benefit of our civilized laws, magicker! You are unworthy to stand against me. But if my people wish to see a trial by battle, they shall have it. I have no fear of a wingless stranger, and I welcome the chance to kill you with my own hands."

She glared at the gathered nobles and spat at Radistha, "Fix this trial for dawn. Then we shall see whose side the gods are on!"

* * *

Immediately after my encounter with the queen, I was escorted away from the feast by a pair of winged guards. I fully expected them to be under instructions to toss me into another miserable prison cell. Instead I was only conducted back to Kinhira's home, where it seemed I would be permitted to spend my last night before the judicial combat.

Nonetheless, the guards stationed themselves outside the home. Clearly no chances were to be taken that I might suddenly decide to toss everything aside and run for my life. I halfheartedly wondered if I stood any chances of besting the guards if I took them by surprise, but didn't seriously entertain the idea. I had as much reason to stay as before. Every soul back in Swiftsfell was depending on me. They just didn't know it.

Kinhira didn't return with me, and it was hours before he finally stepped through the door. Finding his daughter and me on the cushions before the fire where I had just been relating to Tadra the events of the night, he dropped a canvas sack at my feet.

"What is this? I asked. "Where have you been all this time?"

He explained that Radistha had needed him to make many arrangements for tomorrow's trial. He had also given instructions for my preparation.

"I don't understand. What have I to prepare for?" I asked, opening the mouth of the sack and peering inside. In the bottom rested a black metal band, remarkably similar to the one already clasped around my ankle.

"Use that item well," said Kinhira, "and it will be the key to your victory."

"How so?"

"Queen Viranathi has placed certain rules on tomorrow's trial, one of them being that the 'wingless magicker' may not use any of her unnatural powers to achieve victory. If you do so, any win will be invalidated. To ensure that you respect the rule, you will be required to fight with your nathamite band in place."

My heart sank as I felt any hope I'd had of victory slip away. "And because one nathamite shackle does not hamper me enough, she sends a second one?"

He shook his head. "This gift comes from Radistha, not the queen. Take a closer look."

Obediently I upended the sack, letting its contents clatter on the floor. In the flickering firelight, I now noticed subtle differences between the new band and the one I currently wore. This one was thicker, heavier. And when I scratched it, my fingernail left behind a small streak of silver where the black coloring flaked away.

Kinhira said, "I've sent for someone to bring the necessary tools and remove the nathamite band to replace it with this false twin. I've also bribed the guards outside to let him pass. They have no love for Queen Viranathi, and their orders are to keep you indoors, not to bar the entrance of others. With any luck, our deception will go unnoticed tomorrow, and your only challenge during the trial will be to survive long enough to defeat the queen by means of some subtle magic. Remember that whatever tricks you use must be invisible to the spectators or you will forfeit your victory and do your Swiftsfell friends no good."

I poked at the false shackle. "Radistha's plan is a solid one, but I cannot go through with it."

I was as surprised by my decision as Kinhira and Tadra were, but I knew the moment I said the words that they were right and I would stand by them. What I did not know was how to make the others see my reasoning. It wasn't as if I had ever cared in the past whether I won a fight fairly, as long as I got the outcome I needed. But this time was different. Radistha had agreed on my behalf that I would not violate the accepted regulations, and I was bound by his word. I hated it but saw no choice.

Kinhira tried to change my mind, and we debated long into the night. A stranger came and went, removing my nathamite shackle and replacing it with the false one. I allowed him to do it and joyfully embraced my magic once again, now the barrier between it and me was gone. But I remained determined.

Later, after everyone had given up trying to persuade me and had gone to their beds, I lay awake for a long time, gazing into the coals of the dying fire and wondering if this was my last night to live. The final thing I felt as I drifted off to sleep was the vaguely uncomfortable bite of the false shackle digging into my flesh.

My dreams had not been restful lately, and tonight was no exception. I dreamed of Myria admonishing me and of all the inhabitants of Swiftsfell dying because of my stubborn refusal to use every tool at my disposal to save them. Mixed in were memories of Hadrian in the old days, lecturing me about duty and honor. And Terrac? He faded in and out of my dreams, sometimes appearing as the young man I now knew, other times reverting to the annoyingly self-righteous boy he had been at our first meeting years ago. I awoke more confused than ever.

It was nearly dawn.

Chapter Twelve

The trial took place in a cavernous arena with elevated seating that seemed to hold the entire population of the fortress. The noise of the gathered audience bounced around the walls in a blend of voices, laughter, and shuffling, stamping feet that I tried to close my ears to.

As I waited at the edge of the arena, Drejian guards surrounded me as though my enemies feared I would flee. They weren't far wrong. My mouth was uncomfortably dry as I watched Radistha before me, making a speech to the gathered spectators. I understood only a few words but made out that he was explaining what brought us here and what was at stake for the two combatants.

Kinhira was at my elbow. He had, in fact, stayed with me all morning, and I was grateful to have one supporter at my side. I had never figured out what he thought of me personally, but there was no question that, if only from allegiance to his master, he wanted my victory. That made him the nearest thing to a friend I had in this place.

As the queen came into view, I licked my lips nervously and wondered if I would ever see my real friends again. Would I set eyes on Terrac again? Or was this my last day, my final hour?

An unexpected commotion from behind drew my attention, and I turned to find Tadra pushing her way through the guards to reach my side. After her strange absence all morning, I had thought she might not attend the event, but here she was.

Her face glowed with excitement. "I have brought something to help you," she said mysteriously.

My hopes rose as I saw what it was. "My bow? How did you come by this? I thought it was lost for good."

Looking pleased with herself, she handed it over along with an unfamiliar quiver filled with arrows. These simple arrows of Drejian design looked incongruous next to my beautifully constructed Skeltai bow, but I cared nothing for that.

Tadra said, "I heard your weapons were taken at your capture, and I thought you would fight with more confidence if you had them back."

She didn't know how true that was. Kinhira had helped me choose my weapons earlier—a short sword and wooden shield. The sword had never been my strongest weapon, and I had no experience fighting with a shield nor time to practice with this one. Kinhira had insisted that with the queen's choice of weapon a shield would be a necessity, and I had trusted his advice. But having my own weapons as backup was a tremendous relief.

The instant I closed my fist around the wooden arm of the bow, I felt it vibrate to life beneath my fingers as if it had been waiting for me. As it glowed warmly against my skin, I imagined I could hear its whispered greeting tickling along the edges of my mind.

Just as in the old days, we were one.

With a surge of renewed energy, I accepted my throwing knives, which Tadra had also obtained, and tucked them into their usual places before slinging the bow and quiver across my back.

Kinhira cut into my thoughts. "My master is now explaining the rules of the trial. He says that while neither combatant will use magic to obtain a cheap victory, both are permitted the manmade weapons of their choice. Also, that the fight is to the death and no outside forces will interfere."

Queen Viranathi had begun parading around the arena to the cheers of the crowd. She still wore her royal circlet with its curtain of golden beads trailing down her back and shoulders. But she had exchanged her jewels and scarlet garments for half armor that shielded her breast and abdomen. She had adorned her already bone-tipped wings with more sharp spikes of gold that glinted with her movements, beautiful as they were deadly.

I looked at her formidable build and the muscular wings rising above her shoulders and thought the great trident in her hands was almost unnecessary. She could kill me just as easily with her clawlike fingers or a well-aimed slap of a wing. I banished a quick mental image of Martyn being pierced by Micanthria's wing.

Radistha left off speaking and exited the area. Kinhira's gentle nudge informed me it was time. I realized suddenly that I hadn't offered him or Tadra the thanks I probably owed them for getting me this far. I opened my mouth to do that very thing when I was silenced by the trumpeting of a loud horn that filled the arena and bounced off the rock walls.

The trial by battle had begun.

I met my opponent at the center of the ring, and we circled one another, weapons at the ready. I had never liked fighting against polearms and was hesitant to be the first to attack. My shield was an unfamiliar weight on my left arm, and the short sword was almost as awkward in my other hand, adding to my feeling of unreality.

As if sensing my hesitation, the Drejian queen mocked, "You are weak without your magic, dragon slayer. This hour you will answer for Micanthria's blood with your own."

Never much of a prefight taunter, I ignored her threat and looked for a weak spot in her armor. Under the arm or at the neck was usually good.

Angered by my silence, she continued, "You magicker friends will also pay for your crimes. Too long have I suffered their insolence. When I have finished feeding your entrails to the ravens, I will unleash the might of my winged warriors on Swiftsfell."

For reply, I feinted to the right to get a sense of how she would defend. As I thought, she flared her broad wings as though preparing to take flight. But instead of lifting off the ground, she stood firm and thrust her formidable trident at my torso.

I made another attack, real this time, but didn't make it beyond the length of her weapon. The sharp prongs of the trident bit into the shield I instinctively raised at the last instant. I was startled by the strength of the blow, and my arm throbbed at the hard impact.

Disengaging myself, I caught a glint of cruel pleasure in my opponent's eyes. She could break past my puny defense anytime she pleased, I realized, but she was enjoying prolonging the match.

I launched another assault, and she casually deflected my blade with the haft of her weapon. She beat her broad wings, stirring up the dust of the arena and throwing grit into my eyes, and ascended into the air.

It was the opening I had been waiting for, and I threw down my sword and shield to draw my bow from my shoulder and fire off an arrow at the figure hovering above me. The shaft bounced harmlessly off her breastplate, and before I could loose another, my enemy descended in a fury of wings.

She attacked simultaneously with trident at the front and wings swiping at me from either side. I barely had time to scramble after my shield. My discarded sword was beyond reach. Exchanging my bow for one of the knives tucked up my sleeve, I knew it was a ludicrous match for the trident, but what else could I do?

The trident crashed into my shield, and I planted my feet, shoving back against it with all my strength. Viranathi hadn't expected that, and in her confusion, I got close enough to shove my knife into the gap in her plate mail. A fountain of bright blood spewed from the wound under her arm.

But she seemed not to feel it. Fighting more viciously, she beat back my shield with a series of quick blows that left my forearm numb. I let the clumsy weight slip off my arm and stood before her, all but helpless.

Defend yourself. You know what you must do.

It had been a long time since I had felt the bow's influence nudging at the back of my mind, but it was there now. I thought of the false nathamite I wore around my ankle and almost gave in to the temptation to draw on my magic to save myself.

But I didn't.

One of Viranathi's heavy wings descended, smacking me to the ground. Dazed by the blow, I slid a short distance across the sand. The world dipped and spun around me, and as I crawled to my knees, I became aware of the cheering from spectators on the fringes of the ring. My panting breath rasped loudly in my ears.

I blinked against the salty sweat and grit in my eyes as my enemy's shadow came looming over me. I sensed, rather than saw, her raising her trident for the killing strike. A quick succession of images flashed before my eyes. Brig, my old nemesis Rideon the Red Hand, Terrac…

As the trident fell, I instinctively threw out a hand as if to fend it off and pushed a wave of magic against the Drejian queen. It was the same trick I had used against the dragon, Micanthria, shoving all the fear out of myself and into my enemy.

Viranathi froze as the wall of magic crashed into her, a look of startled terror glazing her eyes. Then she stumbled backward in confusion, her great wings flapping clumsily to lift her off the ground. She retreated high into the air and circled the arena.

Devoid now of fear or any other emotion, I drew my bow and nocked an arrow. I didn't try to control it this time but let the bow direct my aim. I was unaware even of loosing the arrow until I felt the fletching graze my fingers and the tension of the string snapping back.

I didn't see where the arrow struck. One instant Viranathi was swooping through the air, the next she was plummeting downward. I fired more arrows, not even counting how many had time to hit their target before she crashed into the ground.

At her heavy impact, the earth shuddered beneath my feet. Dust swirled around the Drejian queen, and the arena became hushed, silence descending over the spectators. I didn't have to cross the ring to be sure Viranathi was dead. I could feel it in the bow's satisfaction.

Prince Radistha and other officials entered the circle and ran to the motionless body. After a brief examination, Radistha pronounced Queen Viranathi defeated and the wingless magicker the righteous victor. The waiting audience erupted in mingled celebration and protest.

I wiped a dirty forearm across my sweaty brow and sank to the ground to recapture my breath. Adrenaline draining away as swiftly as it had come, I tried to comprehend what had happened. The sense of victory swelling at the edge of my consciousness wasn't my own. For me there was no triumph, no rush of relief. All I could think was that at the crucial moment some instinct of self-preservation had made me draw on my magic despite all my intentions to the contrary.

The false nathamite around my ankle felt unnaturally heavy.

Chapter Thirteen

Immediately after the trial, I was escorted back to Kinhira's home by the Drejian warriors. Seeing my confusion, Kinhira reassured me these guards were only with me now for my safety. The outcome of the trial had, in theory, immediately left me a free person. But there was a high probability not all the trial's spectators would be pleased with the outcome, and some might attempt to avenge Viranathi's death.

Despite Kinhira's assurances, I was uneasy. I did not know Prince Radistha well enough to place much trust in him. I couldn't help but wonder, as I was marched away, if some dark fate was in store for me. What if some of the officials or spectators had noticed my use of illegal magic during the trial? But at least the guards allowed me to keep my weapons. The recent fight had left me so exhausted I wasn't sure I could muster the energy to defend myself if I needed to. But the weight of the bow across my back was reassuring, as was the magic hovering within reach.

It turned out that I had no need of these defenses because the warriors delivered me, as promised, to Kinhira's door. Tadra, who had accompanied me home, ushered me in and tried to make me comfortable. She drew a tub of hot water for my bath and laid out fresh clothes of her own for my use. I could see she was excited to discuss the trial but was too polite to press me for conversation when I was clearly tired. I soaked in my hot bath, feeling the aches and weariness seep from my muscles. All the while, scenes from the trial played through my mind. I couldn't quite bury the guilty knowledge that I had cheated to obtain my victory and worried I would be found out.

Even if I wasn't caught in my deception, what was going to happen to me? Would I really be allowed to go free after killing the Drejian queen? Or, now that his dirty work was done, would Prince Radistha go back on his word? What assurance did I have that he would not betray me as easily as he had his rival?

Kinhira had stayed behind when Tadra and I left the arena, and it was another hour before he returned. By then I was dressed again and had rested as much as my anxious thoughts would allow.

For someone who had taken so long to return home, Kinhira was impatient. He said, "My master has decided you must go at once. You will not spend another night in the mountain."

"What is the great hurry?" I asked. "Is something wrong?"

"Not wrong, exactly," he said. "But some of the queen's supporters are unhappy with the results of the trial and are pressing Prince Radistha to declare the results invalid."

"And what does that mean? Is Radistha going to go back on our agreement?"

Kinhira's expression was offended. "My master will keep his end of the bargain, as you have kept yours. But it is difficult for him to control the actions of others, and it may take some time to bring his enemies in line. Meanwhile, your presence will only increase the tension. It will be easier for him to manage his detractors and transition to his rightful place on the throne without you before the people's eyes, reminding them of the late Queen."

He hesitated. "Besides, your friends are making trouble."

My ears perked up. "What friends?"

"Not an hour ago, a pair of wingless strangers were captured as they attempted to enter our gates by stealth. They claim to have come to rescue you."

My heart beat faster. Could it be?

"Where are they?" I demanded. "They have not been harmed?"

"No. In deference to you, they were merely disarmed and imprisoned. Prince Radistha is prepared to release them to you immediately."

"If the three of us depart quickly and quietly?" I guessed.

He agreed. "I can take you to them now if you are ready."

I said my good-byes to Tadra, thinking with brief regret that I had never got the chance to really know her. I took a quick and final look around the small house that had been my home over these tense few days. Then I followed Kinhira out.

* * *

When my friends stepped out of their dreary dungeon cell, it felt like I was seeing them for the first time in years rather than mere days. I briefly took in Hadrian's weary, travel-stained appearance before reassuring myself that the priest was still as solid as ever. But my eyes slid quickly past him, searching for Terrac. When I found him, relief rushed through me.

Terrac's haggard face showed signs of his recent illness, but his eyes, alarmingly feverish in my visions, were now clear, and he seemed steady on his feet.

I threw myself straight into his arms and was so caught up in the joy of our reunion that it took me a moment to realize how thin he felt. His time in the desert had drained him, and he was lucky to have survived.

"I'm sorry I could not get to you when you needed me," I told him. "I wanted to help when you were ill, but I couldn't escape."

He pulled back a little from my embrace to look into my face. "How did you know what happened to me?"

"I saw you in a dream," I said. "I'll explain later. The important thing right now is that you're alive and you're here."

"Yes, thanks to the most incredible stubbornness I've ever seen," Hadrian put in, clapping a friendly hand down on Terrac's shoulder. "I tried to persuade him to return to Swiftsfell for proper healing. But neither the voice of reason nor death's beckoning hand could deter him from reaching you."

"We were stranded for a long while," Terrac added. "We would have arrived sooner, but after the viper's bite I was very ill and unable to travel for several days. Hadrian stayed by me and eventually nursed me back to health."

"Magicked him to health is more like it," Hadrian said. "And he's still a long way from recovered yet. He belongs in a sickbed."

Terrac ignored that. "As soon as the worst was over and I was back on my feet, we came straight here. After what happened to Myria, I knew you would seek revenge against the Drejians."

"You needn't worry about that. I've settled affairs with the Drejians. Justice has been achieved for Myria, the Drejians will not attack Swiftsfell again, and we are free to walk out of here."

I was tempted to add that I had managed to accomplish all this perfectly well on my own. But seeing Terrac's frail condition, I couldn't bring myself to lecture him for doing exactly what I would have done had our places been reversed. Some other time I would remind him that it had never been my habit to sit helpless, awaiting rescue. But not now. For today, he had risked his life and very nearly lost it in an attempt to save me.

I realized abruptly that I was still in his arms. And considering our last conversation back in Swiftsfell and the way we had decided to leave things, I probably shouldn't be.

Awkwardly, I stepped back and tried to cover my emotion, saying briskly, "Let me see the injury."

I examined his wounded hand, the same hand that had once lost fingers under the knife of a Skeltai shaman. But the site of the bite was heavily bandaged. I caught a glimpse of blue veins, unnaturally raised, spiraling up the pale skin of his wrist to disappear inside his sleeve. The entire arm seemed stiff, and he moved it gingerly.

I would have explored further, but Kinhira, whose presence I had all but forgotten, cut into our reunion. "It would be best to get the three of you to the surface now," he advised.

He was right. I had been confined in this dim world under the mountain long enough. It was time to return to the sunlight.

* * *

Despite Kinhira's assurances that Prince Radistha would keep his part of the bargain, I half expected some attempt to be made at preventing our leaving. Long after we had left the Drejian stronghold and the mountains behind us to travel back toward Swiftsfell, I was still looking over my shoulder. But no winged Drejian figures appeared in the sky. There was no pursuit, and our trek across the wasteland was uneventful.

One night when we made camp at a halfway point, I was startled to realize we were in the exact place I had seen in my visions. The spot where I had seen Terrac's suffering. As I knelt at that shallow pool to refill our waterskins, I had the strange sense of stepping from dream into reality.

Terrac was building a campfire—the desert temperature could drop surprisingly low after sundown. Even though his arm was obviously troubling him and he had to work one-handed, he wouldn't allow anyone to help.

I found myself alone with Hadrian and remembered with a pang that I owed the warrior priest an apology.

"Thank you for looking after Terrac when he was ill," I told him. "I ran out of Swiftsfell without a word to you, and you'd be within your rights to be angry."

Hadrian looked surprised. "My tending Terrac had nothing to do with whether I was angry at you. I did it because it was right and because he is my friend."

"Yes, of course. I only meant—"

He cut me off. "While we're on the subject, why did you leave in such a hurry? I can understand your feelings at losing your grandmother, but that doesn't explain why you didn't come to me and ask for my help."

I could not meet his eyes. How could I tell someone important to me that I hadn't trusted him to do what I needed? "I, um, guess I wasn't thinking clearly." And then, because I knew he could sense the lie, I amended, "I was afraid you might try to persuade me against my rash course. I thought you would call it a foolish, reckless quest."

"Of course it was foolish and reckless." His mouth twitched. "But when has that ever stopped me from supporting you?"

He was right, and I had to laugh.

I walked away, relieved to know that despite my mistake my relationship with Hadrian was right back where it had always been.

But seeing Terrac at work, I quickly remembered I still had fences to mend.

"Let me do that," I said, snatching a long stick out of his hands and snapping it in two for the fire.

"I'm not helpless," he grumbled.

But he didn't stop me from taking over. Even in the cool of the evening, with the sun dipping beyond the horizon, there was sweat on his brow, and he seemed out of breath. I had seen that he continued to tire easily and his arm seemed to pain him often. He absently massaged it now while watching me build up the fire.

When I had finished my task, I said, "You know, I still haven't seen the injury."

He slowly unwound the bandage on his hand.

I almost gasped when I saw the bite area but forced a bland expression. It had never been a pretty hand since the Skeltai had severed those fingers. But now there was a large circle of black and blue like a great bruise covering the back and at its center the twin punctures where the viper's fangs has pierced flesh. Terrac's veins stood out rigidly, dark blue lines traveling as far up his arm as I could see.

"Is it very painful?" I asked, trying to sound casual.

He was watching me. "It was. But most of the pain is gone now, and it just feels numb all the time. Anyway, you haven't seen the worst."

Carefully and with only one hand, he peeled off his shirt, revealing the ugly blue veins extending all the way up his pale arm and into his shoulder. The arm seemed unnaturally thin and withered.

My eyes stung, and I blinked quickly. "Will you lose the use of your arm?"

He shrugged. "Hadrian thinks it will grow no worse. But whether it will improve, we cannot know."

"Well, at least you are lucky to be alive." My voice was falsely cheerful.

"And am I lucky to be maimed, maybe for life?"

I said lightly, "You always were one to whine about little injuries. I'm sure you will be fine in a week or two."

"Even if I'm not, I would do everything the same again if I had to. Except for grabbing that viper, mistaking it for a piece of firewood. I wouldn't do that part over."

"Maybe. But I hate that all this happened on account of me." I hadn't meant to say the words. They just slipped out.

Terrac glanced at me. "Well, what are fiends for?" he asked, dragging his shirt on again.

I winced because it felt like an opening to continue our conversation from before. Neither of us had directly referenced our fight from before the Swiftsfell attack, and I wanted it to stay that way.

So I changed the subject. "I'm going to ask Hadrian how much longer we have to wait for our supper."

"I think he's trying to stay out of the way so we can settle things."

"Really? I didn't know there was anything to settle."

"You aren't going to make this easy, are you?" he asked. "Listen. With all that has happened, I've had time to think about our fight. And I think I understand now why you overreacted to my reports to the Praetor. It was the secrecy of it that made you feel betrayed. I should have told you what I was doing from the beginning."

I stifled annoyance at his description of my "overreaction" and said, "I think enough has been said about this. I would prefer to put it behind us."

"You mean I am forgiven?"

If only it was that easy to restore trust that had been too often betrayed. I swallowed, almost wanting to say yes. But what came out was, "We are friends again, as we used to be. I think that's all I can give right now and all you can fairly ask."

He wasn't pleased at that, I could tell. He said, "In time, it will be like nothing ever happened. You'll love me as before."

I didn't tell him that a little piece of me loved him still. "I don't think so."

"If you give me a chance to prove you can trust me again—"

I did not allow him to finish. "There is one favor I want from you, Terrac. If you are serious about your apology, you could strike any mention of Swiftsfell or its inhabitants from your report to the Praetor. If you must act as his eyes, tell him about the rest of our travels. Anything that happens from here onward. But do not tell of my grandmother or the magicker community here."

Terrac hesitated, and I hated that he did. "It is the kind of thing he will be most eager to hear."

"But who knows the length of his reach or the level of his influence with the praetor of this province?" I protested. "Cros has always been a safe place for my kind. But Praetor Tarius despises natural magickers, and there is no guessing what trouble he might make for the people of Swiftsfell if tales of them reach his ears. He killed my parents years ago. Do you want to be responsible if he brings harm to others?"

Terrac nodded. "All right. I will leave Swiftsfell out of my report. Will that resolve the trouble between us?"

"It will make us friends again."

If it wasn't exactly the answer he wanted, he shook off his disappointment. "Then it is worth it. Friends again."

He offered his good hand, and I shook it, surprised to find myself smiling. Our brief romantic relationship might be over, but at least we had salvaged our friendship, something I was relieved to have back.

"This does not mean I won't be watching you like a hawk in the future," I warned, only half joking. "First this and then that time you stabbed me in the back when I first came to Selbius…"

"That was *years* ago," he protested, and we fell into good-natured bickering while the desert moon rose above.

Chapter Fourteen

Our return to Swiftsfell was greeted with a tepid reception. The magickers had been busily rebuilding after the recent attack on their village, and they were fearful my actions might bring down more Drejian wrath upon them. But I reassured the village head that my destruction of the dragon, Micanthria, and of the Drejian queen would not be met with reprisal.

The announcement that I had negotiated peace with the queen's heir on behalf of the magicker community was met with enthusiasm. Hadrian immediately pledged himself, Terrac, and me to stay some weeks to help with the reconstruction and replanting. This pleased Calder and the other locals so much that, despite their newly limited resources, they threw us a small feast of celebration on our first night back.

After the feast, I slipped away from my friends. There was something I needed to do, something they could not help me with. I stopped briefly at Myria's home, strangely silent and empty now, and left my weapons there. Except for the bow. I brought that, not for protection but because it offered comfort and familiarity that I had need of just now.

I saw a group of barefoot children playing outside one of the neighboring houses, and I paid one of them to act as my guide. She was a dark-haired, agile little girl who scrambled across the village's swinging rope bridges and rocky cliff paths as easily as a young mountain goat. I followed slowly and with more caution.

Dusk was falling, and the first fireflies were twinkling like stars when we left behind the lights and sounds of the village. My small nameless guide led me up a path carved into the side of the rock. It wound upward and was well maintained, with convenient steps and rope railings to prevent a clumsy fall. The girl kept such a brisk pace that I was puffing and out of breath before I reached the end of the arduous ascent, where the path disappeared sharply around an outcropping of stone. The little girl beckoned impatiently until I rounded the outcropping and found myself on the ledge of a deep chasm.

Here beneath the partial shelter of the rocks meeting overhead was Swiftsfell's equivalent to a graveyard. There were rows of niches built into the sides of the cliff, each shelf just long and wide enough to accommodate a single body. Some of these stood empty, awaiting future occupants. Others had been sealed up with the same clay mixture the people used to build their homes, preserving the dead from the elements and whatever scavengers might reach them at these heights.

The little girl showed me to the recess where Myria had been laid to rest, then left me. The niche was freshly sealed up, and chiseled into the rough clay surface was a symbol that I supposed represented Myria.

I traced the inscription with my fingers, thinking that now I was here I did not know what it was I had come to say.

"I wish I had got the chance to know you better," I whispered. "There was a great deal I would have liked to ask you, about my mother, about our family."

To have finally found a living relative only to see her snatched away so soon seemed incredibly cruel. But at least I had avenged her and ensured the ones she loved would have a safer future. There was comfort in that.

So I sat down beside Myria's resting place and told her everything about my journey to the territory of the Drejians. About my defeat of Micanthria, my experiences among the Drejian people, and how the dragon-scale amulet Myria had given me had eventually helped me win the trial by combat and save my life. The augmenter felt heavy around my neck as I confessed how I had cheated and broken my word in order to defeat Queen Viranathi.

I also told about Martyn and how I had promised him as he lay dying that I would locate and watch over his little brother. I still had no notion how I would carry that out but supposed it was a problem that would have to wait until I returned to my own province. As would the mystery of who had hired Martyn, lying to persuade him to destroy me.

It was a relief to pour out so many thoughts I hadn't spoken aloud before.

"And here's another thing," I said into the stillness. "I have my bow back again. Funny how it fell into Martyn's hands and traveled such a distance to make its way back to me. I am not sure how to feel about that. I have been too much influenced by its whims before, but maybe I've grown stronger since then and it will not affect me as it once did."

The bow, resting in its place across my back, grew warm at the mention of its name, and its soft glow filled the empty chasm. I realized darkness had fallen. The rocks above blotted out the moonlight, and there was only the golden illumination of the bow to light my way.

Feeling an urge to return to the warmth and companionship of my friends, I said a final farewell to Myria and made my way out of the chasm.

Not an Ending,
But a Resting Place

The cries of the gulls soaring overhead break into my thoughts. Until we arrived at the coast, I had never seen seabirds or imagined the vastness of the ocean now stretched before me. I am still awed by the sight, even though I have traveled far these last few months and seen so many new things.

After departing Swiftsfell, Terrac, Hadrian, and I spent the following seasons visiting all the provinces. We saw the snow-capped mountains of Kersis and the forested hills of Camdon. Wherever we went, Hadrian looked for magicker communities and asked for their stories and histories, cataloguing them in his book, which has grown very thick.

And when we finished our tour of the provinces, we set out for the kingdom itself—Lythnia. To reach it, we had to cross the mountains of Arxus, reentering Drejian territory. But although I felt a pang of unease at their nearness, we had no trouble from the Drejian people.

Now, walking along the moonlit shore of the Lythnian coast with the pebble-strewn beach beneath my feet and the roar of the ocean in my ears, I set aside thoughts of Drejians and everything else I've experienced over the past year. The future looms ahead, and with it the end of my freedom approaches. The Praetor's words ring in my head.

"One year hence, you will return to my service and take up the duties I set before you."

My time is almost past, and I will soon return to my province. There is no question of breaking my oath to the Praetor, for if I did, my friends would surely suffer for it. I have only a few weeks of freedom left. Hadrian wants to spend that time studying the magickers of this new region, for he has heard rumors of powerful dryads living in the near forest of Treeveil.

But home beckons, and my mind drifts from this foreign place. In my head, I pretend I'm walking shady, forested paths and breathing the mingled pine and earth scents of Dimmingwood. I am ready to go back.

Ilan's journey continues in spring 2015 with Book VI, Rule of Thieves. Until then, explore the kingdom of Lythnia in the new Catalysts of Chaos series.

ABOUT THE AUTHOR

C. Greenwood started writing stories shortly after learning her ABCs and hasn't put down her pen since. After falling in love with the fantasy genre more than a decade ago, she began writing sword and sorcery novels. The result was the birth of her best known works, the Legends of Dimmingwood series. In addition to her writing, Ms. Greenwood is a wife, mom and graphic designer.

Want to learn more about C. Greenwood or her books? Check out her website or "like" her on Facebook.

Legends of Dimmingwood Series

Magic of Thieves ~ Book I
Betrayal of Thieves ~ Book II
Circle of Thieves ~ Book III
Redemption of Thieves ~ Book IV
Journey of Thieves ~ Book V
Rule of Thieves ~ Book VI

Catalysts of Chaos Series

Mistress of Masks ~ Book I
Betrayer of Blood ~ Book II
Summoner of Storms ~ Book III

Other Titles

Dreamer's Journey

Made in the USA
San Bernardino, CA
22 January 2016